NOT TO KEEP

A Brother's Story

From WW1 to the Great Depression
and the
1935 Hurricane

A Florida Novel by

Rebecca J. Johnston

For information regarding permission, please write to:
info@barringerpublishing.com
Barringer Publishing, Naples, Florida
www.barringerpublishing.com

Illustrations by Henry H. Johnston
@henryh.johnston on Instagram

Cover and layout by Linda S. Duider
Cape Coral, Florida

ISBN: 978-1-954396-04-3
Library of Congress Cataloging-in-Publication Data
Not to Keep: A Brother's Story
Rebecca J. Johnston

Printed in U.S.A.

To Rosie, who has lost more than any
country deserves to ask.

"We are the sacrifice."

———

Sons of Ulster marching towards the Somme.

Contents

FOREWORD

I first met Rebecca Johnston through our mutual interest in all things Hemingway and got to know her through our involvement in the formation and nurturing of the Florida Hemingway Society. Anyone who knows Rebecca should not be the least bit surprised that her first novel has a connection to the famous author. But perhaps a better way to describe how Hemingway is connected to this story is to say there is an intersection with the writer. Because this is not a story about Hemingway or any other famous person. Instead, it is a story about the lives, loves, tragedies and triumphs of ordinary people who are not famous in the way we think of fame in today's hyped up social media, twenty-four hour news cycle, frenzy.

Instead, this is a story about ordinary people doing extraordinary things. They live in towns where the ponds are named Watermelon, and they live on streets where everyone knows and looks out for one another.

The other way Hemingway has seeped into this book-these stories, is the way in which Rebecca has taken his advice. Write what you know, Hemingway often said. While he wasn't the first to suggest it, he believed in it as an absolute requirement for good writing.

These characters and the stories they are living are real because they are honest. They are honestly portrayed and they are honestly revealed. The author has done her best to use her knowledge and the experiences she has garnered to breathe life into them and to show them with all their strengths and weaknesses. It is this dedication, translated into words that will ultimately transport you into their world.

I have referred to the characters in this book as ordinary people doing extraordinary things. I may have gotten the characterizations backward. The people you are about to meet, might best be described as extraordinary people doing what we have all come to expect as ordinary things. Going to war, surviving great hurricanes, sacrificing everything for loved ones and sometimes strangers, and yes, making mistakes and living with lifelong regrets.

As you get to know Mil, Caleb, Ricky, Rosie and the others, you can make your own decision as to whether or not they are ordinary or extraordinary. One thing's for sure, if it weren't for them and millions of people like them who have made sacrifices, sometimes the ultimate sacrifice, our lives would be much different. Thank you, Rebecca, for taking us on this journey.

~ Michael Curry

PREFACE

In 2017, after having recently finished my masters' thesis on Hemingway and the Soća Front, I came across a call for papers for a conference at Santa Fe College in Gainesville, Florida titled *Hemingway: Between Key West and Cuba*. I began thinking of Hemingway topics I would enjoy researching and writing on for this conference and quickly settled on Hemingway and the Labor Day Hurricane of 1935, which is seen in Hemingway's novel *To Have and Have Not*. I was both hired to teach at Santa Fe and accepted to present my research on Hemingway and his hurricane within a few weeks. I threw myself into researching the veterans who were neglected by the US government and left to die in the Keys. These men were truly at the heart of Hemingway's novel. They were men who were rejected for their inability to bounce back from their war experiences and provide for their families without government assistance. Hemingway was able to make a living from writing and thus he was separate from them, but he was connected to them.

I presented my research that summer to an intimidating audience that included Jackson Sasser who was at the time the president of Santa Fe College, Valerie Hemingway, and

Raul Villarreal, whose father worked for Hemingway, who all graciously shared kind words about my presentation. After the conference I spoke with my dear Aunt Anne Hughes who told me she thought one of her twin uncles had lost his life in the Labor Day Hurricane. The thought of my great uncle losing his life in the hurricane I had just studied fascinated me and I knew I had to tell their story, and in doing so to tell the story of all of the forgotten veterans who died in the Keys due to government neglect.

A parallel story had been brewing in my mind for several years. I had been running with a dear friend whose fiancé and brother were both Marines who had lost their lives one day apart in Iraq, leaving her a young widow and single mother of an infant. She is one of the strongest women I know, and she never lets her losses hold her down in life, but she also does not forget her losses or their sacrifices. One year after attending a local Memorial Day ceremony we were discussing the ceremony's focus on law enforcement officers, firefighters, and veterans. Her heartbroken question of "I remember them everyday, why can't everyone else remember them just one day a year?" was one I could not forget. Truly these two men deserve to be remembered, as do all men and women who have lost their lives in service of the country. As I started this novel, I knew that Ricky Lord and Caleb Powers would be a focus. While they are not their characters, as I was not fortunate enough to know them, their names are used to remind readers of the real sacrifice Ricky and Caleb made, and the sacrifice put on the woman they loved and left behind.

ACKNOWLEDGEMENTS

Despite Paul Simon's song to the contrary, no man is an island. Taking it a step further, no book is written solely on the strength of the author. This novel would not have come into being without the constant support and encouragement of my husband, Lt. BJ Johnston whose love, advice, companionship, and support has helped me accomplish everything I have done in my life, and whose adventuresome spirit has brought me to places on this globe I never thought I would see. I would also like to thank my children, their spouses, and my grandson for all of their kind words of support. Mia and Louis, Bobby and Hannah, Micaiah, Lexi, and Ed, Henry and Sydney, and Nina, you are truly the greatest joys in my life. Mandy Reed was consistently willing to read over drafts, offer advice, and even open her home to me for writing weekends. Aunt Anne Hughes was an inspiration and a constant source of encouragement. Fawn Owens offered knowledge and encouragement. Josh Dease, Bobby and Micaela Warren, and Henry Johnston of *The Finer Things Club* were the first to read chapters and offer words of support and advice for improvements. K9 Officer Scott Wiggins was kind enough to teach me how to hide a body in the woods. Erin Hughes helped me as I navigated the world of queries. And finally, a heartfelt acknowledgement for the artist, and my friend, Raul Villarreal, who made me think I could.

INTRODUCTION

Plans do not often work out as well as they seem they will, and that is often the case with writing. A story once begun takes on a life of its own as characters do what they will. As I began researching the lives of my great uncles, I discovered not much was known about their lives and deaths and only one living relative knew anything about them. No known pictures exist in my family. War service, date of birth and date of death is unknown for both. My paternal grandfather, however, did serve in World War One. Records of his registration, training, deployment and return home do exist. In creating a novel to bring light to the lives of the men who sacrificed at the nation's behest in World War One I realized there are a host of men who served whose lives will never be known and yet their stories need to be told. With this thought in mind, I twined together the unknown lives of my great uncles and what I did know of my grandfather, and Will and Mil took shape. Twins were often given rhyming names at the turn of the twentieth century, so their first names were kept to reflect the cultural oddity of their day and age. What I did not know of their lives I filled in with research. World War One is of particular interest to me as my paternal grandmother was the kind of loving, cookie-making grandmother one would never want to forget. Perhaps in researching her husband's war, I felt I knew her a bit more. My undergraduate degree is partially in Modern European History and my research into WWI continued into my literary studies for my masters and now my doctorate. There is a host of information to study, and I hope that in the creation of this story I have told the story well.

The issue initially was how to tell Ricky, Caleb, Mil and Will's stories together. As I pondered both stories, I saw a common thread. The men lost in the Labor Day Hurricane had served their country, just as Ricky and Caleb had. As a nation we encouraged these young men to do their patriotic duty and go off to war. In the case of the veterans in the WPA camps in the Keys, they were not received well in the years following their return as is evidenced by the governmental response to the Bonus Army. As a society we both asked these men to serve and then rejected the outcome of that service. In the case of Ricky and Caleb, while they lost their lives serving their country, as a country we cannot consistently remember them even on Memorial Day. In these two ideas I saw the need for us as a nation, as communities, as churches, and as individuals to reconsider how we receive veterans upon their return home and how we support our war widows and widowers, and thus the united story was born.

PROLOGUE

This story is set in rural North Central Florida, in a county that is still wild and wonderful—the true Florida. The characters live and exist along the banks of the Suwannee River, where they grow up with a Tom Sawyer like childhood. The cities of Chiefland, then Hardeetown, and Cedar Key are real cities worth a visit, and the characters are a representation of the honest, hard-working, and tight-knit communities that exist in these towns even to this day. While I could not do them justice, I hope I have made them proud.

CHAPTER ONE

Reasons Why

There's so much work to be done for the dead. Initially, there's just the body to worry about and if someone died legal like, that ain't a problem. Call the authorities, call the funeral home, call a doc if'n ya ain't sure. Lord knows I dealt with more than my share of bodies, but not with your daddy. Your daddy is what showed me the importance of havin' a body after. With your daddy, there were so many bodies, but not his. Tried as I might, but there never was nothin' ta find. Anne, there are things to be fixed which can't be fixed, but I aim to try.

Only a few mistakes in life can't be undone. Fail at a job? Try another. Lord knows I've had plenty. Lose your house? Start savin' for another. Many of us did. But if your mistake leads to someone's death, that can't be undone. See, Anne, your daddy was the way he was because of me and because of so many others. I want you to see who he was. He was my twin, and I miss him like a part of me has been sawed off. Mostly I try not to think of it, but today it's been ten years since he was gone, and so I pick up the grief, dust it off, and sit with another drink for a while. The grief is always there like a heavy coat I can't and don't want to take off, but on days like today, the coat is what I'm lookin' at.

Doc tells me I don't have long—cirrhosis of the liver, or somethin' like that. There's so much you don't know. Mil and I didn't ever talk about it, and your mama, she was too much of a lady to talk about what she knew. So today, I'll drink and write you, dear Anne. Remember your daddy as he was, and maybe in rememberin', forgive him for what he became—for what we became.

For this anniversary, I've come back to where it all ended. I've come back to the Florida Keys. Sittin' and lookin' out at the water, I wonder where he is. They never found him, or a lot of the other guys. I'm goin' ta write from Key West tonight. Gonna remember all those weekends we had. I hope in these letters you can see the war broke us and we couldn't be made whole again. But let me start at the beginnin'.

CHAPTER TWO

New Friends

I suppose I should start with how Mil and I met Caleb, Ricky, and Rosie. They came before your mama, and without them our childhood woulda been pretty dull. You see, there used'ta be this spot out back of Caruso's land, had a pond we called Watermelon Pond. Some story went 'round 'bout the first white folks to settle Chiefland throwin' watermelons in at the end of melon harvestin' time. Sounds like a way to get rid of overripe melons to me, but what do I know. We never harvested melons on our land.

Well, by the time we was young boys, there weren't no

melons in Watermelon Pond, and the year before we started school there weren't no water in the pond, neither. Have you ever walked on the bottom of a dried pond or lake? Well, the water isn't really gone. It's like what's left of it sort of shaked into the mud and the mud can't hold it all. It gets real dark, and then it cracks. The top layer gets dry, but underneath it's all puddin' like. That day, Mil and I snuck out to the pond and we could walk on the top of these large columns of mud, maybe one, two feet high, that formed between the cracks all over the bottom of the pond. We couldn't walk from one column to the next, because the mud in the cracks was very wet and it could suck the shoes right offa your feet never to be seen again; we had to hop from one column to the next, and when we landed on a new column, it would jiggle with one of us on top of it and we'd struggle to stay standin' because we knew if we fell in that mud, mama would skin us alive, or at least make us do the washin'—a chore which neither of us relished. Well, we was hoppin' from one mud pile to the next and laughin' at the mud shakin' under us when we heard laughin' from behind us. There stood these three kids. Two of 'em were mirror images of each other, exceptin' for Caleb's height—that was Rosie and Caleb Howard. Guy was like a lanky, string bean, in fact we used'ta tell him he got that way by eatin' too many of his mama's green beans. Both Rosie and Caleb had straw color hair, and Rosie's hair was always leadin' the way, gettin' where she was goin' before her head got there. And then there was Ricky Murle. He was the kinda guy who always stood out, even as a little boy. He wasn't taller than everybody else, he just looked like he was. He stood out, his height dwarfed by his muscles, even at a young age. Don't known how that came to be, but I knew at first glance that we was goin' ta be friends. Maybe somethin' about his eyes, which always seemed like they was laughin' at some joke the rest of us hadn't heard yet.

Well, there they was, watchin' us and wantin' in on the fun. Rosie yelled out to see if it was safe. The three of them was in all white; they'd just come from some church baptism in the river nearby. Folks all wore white to baptisms then. At that point, we'd never been to a church baptism, or a church, but the Murles and Howards saw fit to change that after the mud day.

Ricky and Caleb was always competitive, even from the start, so they yelled out askin' if we wanted to race to the other side of the pond, and of course we did. We all lined up, not even knowin' each others' names. Caleb insisted we line up by height, he seemed to think that would give him some kinda advantage bein' as he was the tallest of us. Unfortunately for him, at that point in his life his height made him kinda awkward like. Guy couldn't keep his balance to save his life. Rosie counted down, and we all started jumpin' from one pile of mud to the next. It was slow goin' because once we landed on one mud pile, we had to wait for it to stop jigglin' before we could jump to the next one. Ricky was the front runner. Your daddy got it in his head that he would make one big leap and he would beat Ricky to the end, but what he didn't see comin' was the big rock covered in mud. He leapt right at it and wrenched his ankle, and with that, fell headfirst into the mud. We all froze. We didn't know each other then, but they all sensed that Mil would be in a lotta trouble for gettin' all covered in mud. The mud had such a powerful suck that he couldn't even get up. He rolled over a bit deeper into the wet, muddy crack he'd fallen into next to the rock. We all started hoppin' over to Mil, but it was slow and he'd taken a slightly different path than me and the other guys, so we had to change course to get to him. Rosie got there first and when she tried to pull him out, she fell in headfirst, so now two of us was covered in mud. The mud got all entrenched in her hair right fast. Girl looked a fright. In the end, all of us was muddy. We couldn't help laughin', all muddy as we was. Well, Mil, he couldn't walk right so we had to carry him out piggyback like. Fortunately, Mil was a small boy back then. Didn't really grow to the size of the rest of us 'til we was young men. Mama said it had somethin' ta do with his birth, but we were born the same day, so I never understood that. Anyways, even Rosie took a turn carryin' Mil out that day. We had a long way to go, hoppin' from firm mud to firm mud with Mil on someone's back, and we laughed the whole way. Turns out Ricky's parents saw Ricky's actions as kind and heroic. He may have left out the part where he was in on the fun, and focused on the savin' part, embellishin' his part in gettin' Mil outta the mud with his twisted ankle and all. Unfortunately, we had to fess up to the whole story to our folks, and then we had to do the washin' for a week, but it was worth it. That day we gained three friends who would mean the most to us in life, aside from your mama, but she didn't come in until much later. I think this is what started Ricky's parents takin' a shine to us. From then on, we were invited to their house and their church. Mil liked church more than I did, but we both liked Ricky's mama's cookin'. They was better off than us, so they had nice dinners every Sunday. From then on, we was inseparable. Did everything together, if we could. But we didn't always get along. Ricky was a little bit better at runnin' and jumpin' and so it was a goal for me, Caleb, and Mil to beat him at anything.

CHAPTER THREE

Huntin'

I always liked chasin' squirrels, and when we was boys, I had the best squirrel huntin' dog. Mil liked to call her his, but I picked her up off the side of the road when she was just a pup, and she never forgot that. She was mine, not ours. That's how things work with brothers when they's kids. It's mine or yours—it ain't ours. Anyways, I named the dog Daisy seein' as she had a white spot on her forehead shaped like a flower. Daisy'd spend hours out in the woods with me and Mil. She'd walk us to school every day and wait to walk us home after. Chiefland was all dirt roads then, so she spent most of her waitin' time just a rollin' in the dirt—got real dirty every day, but Mama liked her walkin' us home, so she didn't mind the dirt Daisy brought in the house too awful much.

Mama and Daddy had a two-room house up on blocks like most of us in the woods did, and Caleb and Rosie lived in the woods near us. Both of us had gone with the ever popular whitewashed look, and Mama made us whitewash that house every summer. Said it built character. Didn't see why we needed to, seein' as it weren't really our house. We was rentin'. I guess Rosie and Caleb's parents saw it different, since they didn't have to whitewash their house too awful much. Their house had only one room, so they was usually lookin' ta get out, even if it meant helpin' us whitewash. I remember one summer we had to paint with that watery whitewash and boy was it hot out. It was hell hot, as my daddy used to say. Felt like 100 degrees burnin' right down on us from the sun and the gnats, those little annoyin' "no-see-ums," started light'n in on us. Caleb decided the gnats didn't bite if'n ya had some of that there paint on your body. That was all we needed. We was covered within' minutes. We was all laughin' and white when Mama came back from the store. She sent us right on down to the river to get cleaned up. Didn't really come off for days, but we kept goin' swimmin', tryin' ta get it off. No bugs bit us neither, so maybe there was some truth to Caleb's idea.

Anyways, Ricky was different. His family lived in town. Lots of those houses had plenty of rooms and more than one floor and big porches to set out on. Not sure what Mr. Murle did—businessman maybe. It's funny the things you forget.

Ricky's dad had more'n we did, but we hunted together all the same. After school most days, Daisy would be waitin' for the lot of us. She was good at blazin' a scent trail. The guys and I would tear outta school with Daisy. Rosie wanted to go, too, but when we was huntin', Daisy was the only girl we took in the woods then. Daisy'd have a fox squirrel treed by the time we caught up with her. Ricky was the best shot, but his family didn't eat squirrel. Maybe that's why we always took him. Mil didn't really hunt. He'd sit his skinny self down in some little hollow in a tree and we'd leave him there. His favorite tree was all hollowed out like his own little cubby hole. Guy weren't afraid of bugs and spiders and such. Wouldn'ta caught me crawlin' in that tree, but your daddy sure did. He'd sit there the whole time we was gone, and when me and the guys'd come back, he'd be there with a story he wrote, a book he read or somethin' he drew. Sometimes, we'd build a fire and skin the squirrels and cook 'em so we could eat and Mil would read us his story. He wrote one for your mama once. Not sure he ever told her, but he read it to us one day when we was huntin'. The story told about a little boy out fishin'. He caught the biggest fish you'd ever seen, pulled it right outta the old Suwannee and carried that fish in his shirt all the way back to camp. He was sure proud to show his dad. When the boy gutted the fish, there was a whole 'nother fish inside of it. When he cut that fish open, there was another fish inside of it. So, the boy got three fish for dinner that night. Wishful thinkin' on Mil's part. He was never good at fishin', and I'm not sure why he thought your mama would like that story.

Anyways, in the summer, the four of us guys would get Ricky's dad to drop us off near the river. He was the only dad that had a car, so we was always hopin' he'd drop us off and save us some walkin'. Well, Caruso had land up there near the river. Man owned half the county, it seemed. He had more land than he knew what to do with, and he was never out in the summer. We'd sneak in at night and set up camp at the springs near the Suwannee. The springs was at the end of a long road, but we'd have to walk in through the woods so as not to get caught. After that long walk, we'd strip to our skivvies and jump in. You never did feel water so cold and clean as that. Takes the breath right outta ya. Mil was the last in every time. The rest of us would race to see who could get in first, or who could jump the farthest. Ricky'd grab handfuls of the moss growin' on trees and mix it with algae floatin' on the water and jam it all together inta these shit bombs, he'd call em. He'd pelt those things at Mil 'til he'd finally get in. We didn't have swimmin' lessons. Even Ricky, whose daddy could've afforded 'em. There was no one to teach us. We just figured it out, like we did everything else. We'd race up and down those springs, course it was harder comin' back up. The current was somethin' else. Guess that's what made us good swimmers.

We'd fish in Caruso's springs, and we'd hunt in his woods. The springs gave us fish to eat and water to drink. That's probably why mama and daddy sent us up there. We came back full and clean every time, and usually we came back with fish to share. On hot days, we'd get up there early and go gator huntin'. The gators would sun themselves on the shore of the river. They didn't like the cold, clear water of the springs, but they sure did like the river. They're creatures of habit. Like to sun in the same spot. We'd spend a few days fishin' and huntin' and spyin' on the gators, then we'd come back for 'em early one mornin'. You see, if you stab 'em between the eyes, they're done for. There's an art to gator huntin'. One summer, we found this big ol' mama gator. Found her nest. They get pretty ornery when they've got a nest. Well, we all wanted this gator, but Mil and me was a bit afraid. Ricky, though, Ricky could get you to do anything and Caleb was always up for a challenge. So, Ricky got Caleb to sneak up and get that gator's attention. He had decided before leavin' the house that a mama gator would want to eat a chicken, so he'd brought this chicken in a sack. A livin' chicken, mind you. He waited 'til the wind was blowin' right and Caleb brought that chicken on up to the gator, sneakin all the way, but when he got there the chicken was too scared to get out of the sack, so Caleb, he started struttin' 'round like a rooster just a-crowin'. It was somethin' else seein' that lanky boy just a-struttin' and a-crowin'. Guess the gator thought so too, cuz that gator made noises I'd never heard a gator make before. But it worked— she never saw my knife a-comin'. Got that bitch between the eyes. Course, I couldn't actually get too close to her, so I'd attached my knife to the end of a pole, real firm like. It did the trick. Let me tell you, that mama was fourteen feet long. Biggest thing we ever did see. Now we were in trouble. We weren't supposed to be on Caruso's land. How were we gonna get that gator out on our backs? It's one thing to carry a little Mil out, it's another to carry out a small dinosaur. Well, Ricky was always the fastest, but at that point Caleb liked to think he was the fastest, and Ricky didn't feel like runnin', so Caleb ran all the way to town to get our daddies. When they heard him tell how big that gator was, they didn't believe him. Thought he was tellin' tales. Poor Caleb. He got 'em ta pile inta Ricky's daddy's car anyways. The look on their faces when they got there was somethin' else. Well, that gator was too big for one car, and we had to park pretty far out, hop a fence and walk a mile or so to get to where the gator was. We needed help, that was for sure. And we didn't want Caruso or the game wardens findin' us. They had themselves some rules for gator huntin' and we liked them to keep them rules to themselves. Ol' Warden Parker had caught us out poachin' turkeys the fall before, and Warden Miller caught us takin' crabs from Faircoth, so they had us in their sights. Miller was a big guy, both in height and in weight. He'd lost an eye in a huntin' accident and made it his life goal to stop other guys from poachin' and losin' an eye, too. I wasn't too worried about him. He was too fat to run fast. But Parker, that guy could run and his scent dog could tree any man, so we had to get this gator out without alertin' the authorities. Ricky's dad decided us boys needed to stay there and cut the thing up inta smaller pieces and he'd take my dad and Caleb's dad down to the bar for reinforcements. There was only one bar in town then, and it was run by the Goodwin family. They was a bit high and mighty for a family runnin' a bar. Guess they sold booze but didn't drink it. Their daughter was about the prettiest thing I'd ever seen, but I didn't get to see much of her. She was too good for us boys in the school, so her daddy hired her a private teacher all the way from Gainesville. Anyways, Goodwin was too good for his patrons, but his bar keep, Dan, he was another thing. I guess he was the go between for Chiefland and the Goodwins. And he ran it right. Every man in town was there at least two or three nights a week and our dads were countin' on that. Now Dan, he didn't let Miller and Parker in there. Said it was bad for business. I guess our daddies cleared that bar out. They came back that night with a single file line of men. They all came with somethin' ta carry off meat with. Daddy left the head of the gator as a sign to Miller and Parker that we'd been there. Couldn't go back there for months, but it was worth it.

We left with lots of gator meat. Dan had given Miller and Parker a tip that us boys had been in Goodwin's earlier braggin' about robbin' Faircloth's crab traps that night. The wardens cleared right out of town to go catch us in the act and while they were spyin' on those traps, all of us snuck the gator back inta town. We had a big town-wide, gator cook off—except for the Goodwins, of course. Those were hungry days in Levy County. A man's silence could be bought with a full belly and some gator meat to take home for the next day. By the time the wardens got back in town, the meat was gone and no one was talkin'. Of course, eventually they found the head and suspected what had happened, but no one was talkin' and the evidence was all eaten or burned and buried.

Us guys, we all kept a claw. Made 'em inta necklaces and wore them off to the war when we was older. Mine really impressed the Italian girls. Saw me as some sort of savage, I guess. Ricky and Caleb's came back from the war, but I never did get Mil's back. That's how it goes sometimes.

Anyways, I'm getting ahead of myself. Gator huntin' we did when it was hot, but in the rainy season, we went frog giggin'. Caleb, he was the best frog gigger. That boy, he could feed an army with frogs and I'm pretty sure he did at some point, if you believe the stories men tell. Well, the summer we was fourteen was a rainy summer at the end of a very dry May. Mama had gotten real sick that winter tryin' ta bring another baby inta this world. Mil and I, we took to the woods even more around that time. We could hear ourselves think in the woods, and Caleb and Ricky usually came, too. Ricky's family didn't need the food, he just came for the sport and more often than not he sent us home with his share of the hunt. Well, this one week in June, it rained every day. The springs lost their clear turquoise color as the river overflowed her bends and filtered inta the springs. Mosquitoes the size of birds started showin' up as soon as the rain stopped and so did the frogs. Now, these frogs had legs the size of chicken wings, and they made a good meal all fried up. The plan was to meet on Caruso's land, just outside of Chiefland, a good space from his house, but not quite to the springs. All the land was marshy after the rains, so we knew the frogs would be out. We went separately at night, so Miller and Parker wouldn't see us. Parker had a house one street over from the road that ended on Caruso's land, so we was all careful to avoid the main road and walk along smaller dirt roads instead. We walked by the light of the moon. The roads were lime-rock and sand then, so the surface of the road was lit up reflecting the light of the moon. When Mil and I got there, Caleb was already there with Rosie, who was wearin' her dad's trousers with her hair all pulled back and stickin' out awkwardly.

"Whatcha bring a girl for," Mil asked. "She's just gonna slow us down." I can still see his confused face, with his brown eyebrows all wrinkled up like caterpillars. Man always did have bushy brows, not that we cared none. Well, Caleb swore that Rosie was the one who taught him to frog gig, and like I said, Caleb was the best frog gigger we knew, so this news came as a surprise for us boys. Ricky was impressed, but we all doubted. Thought Caleb's dad made him take her. Rosie, she stood there, nose in the air, defyin' all of us to try and stop her. Lookin' back, this is likely the night Ricky fell hard for Rosie. She was his whole world, but I'm gettin' ahead of myself again.

Ricky had brought four pairs of waders. He gave his to Rosie, cuz he was wantin' ta see how a girl could gig frogs, so he had to stay in the shallow area of the marsh the river had created when it swelled up. That meant Ricky was our gator look out. Gators like to eat those big ol' frogs too, likely not a big gator but big enough to drown us, so Ricky stood ready, as he always did. Well, Rosie had used her knife to fiddle down an oak stick inta a spear of sorts and she just put those waders on and sallied out inta the dark water with no fear. Us

16

boys, we just followed her in. Mil and I, we had brought our canvas sacks so we started stabbin' those frogs with our spears we brought from home and throw'n 'em inta the sacks. We went to the left towards the Suwannee, and Caleb and Rosie they went to the right towards the springs. Ricky stayed treed, with a light shinnin', so he could keep an eye out. Me and Mil was supposed to get as close to the river as we could without swimmin' and Caleb and Rosie was supposed to get as close to the springs as they could without swimmin', and then we'd circle back and see who got the most frogs. It was always a competition with us. Well, me and Mil felt pretty good 'bout our catch. Musta had fifty or sixty frogs between us. We'd be eatin' frog legs all week and that was okay with us. When we got back to Ricky's light, we could just make out Caleb carryin' a big ol' sack, but Rosie, she didn't have none, so we knew we had 'em beat and Rosie'd been fibbin'. We laughed at Rosie, teasin' her for sayin' she was good at frog giggin' when she didn't even get herself one frog. Mil and me was already celebratin' our victory and laughin' at Caleb, and Caleb just stood there shakin' his head at us. Rosie hadn't even brought a sack, so how did she even think she was gonna be able to compete? You can't hold a spear in one hand and more than a frog or two in the other. Finally, Caleb interrupted our revelry with the announcement that Rosie doesn't bring sacks cuz they ain't big enough for her. Ricky came over then and shined his light on Rosie, and Rosie, she just stood there a grinnin' and started pullin' frogs outta her waders. That girl musta filled those waders with a hundred frogs or more. She walked all the way to town with 'em in her waders, too, when we was all done. That's why we liked Rosie. She wasn't afraid to get dirty none. She came with us huntin' pretty much regular after that. She was a darn good shot but that was Ricky's doin'. He started teachin' her out back of his dad's house; her dad didn't mind seein' that in the country a girl's gotta be able to defend herself, and for Ricky it meant spendin' time with Rosie, but that wasn't what he called her. When she was out with us boys, she was Francis. Ricky said it was her alter ego and more bad ass than the name Rosie. Caleb said it was her middle name, but anyways, she was a different girl when she was with us than when she was with the girls in town, and although Ricky loved both Rosie and Francis, the name change helped us see her as one of the guys. Maybe that was what Ricky wanted at the time.

Anyways, we hauled so many frogs inta town that night the whole town had frogs for days. Course there weren't many of us livin' in Chiefland back then. We sure did eat good, though. Nothin' like a frog leg fried up with some heart of palm next to it.

CHAPTER FOUR

The Darkness

Most of the time, we hunted pigs, frogs, deer, and gator. Sometimes we hunted men, but only with good reason. This is where your mama comes in. It was June, I think. I remember the day clearly, but the date slips my mind sometimes. Your dad would have remembered. Well, that year there was an incident. The guys and I had been out fishin' all weekend. Rosie didn't come with us on those overnight trips then. We'd gone out on the river and not come back 'til we had enough fish. Caleb always said there were never enough fish, but once we couldn't carry anymore in our canoes, we said it was enough for the time bein'.

Well, we came back and were droppin' off Caleb seein' how his house was first and he said he'd caught more of the fish. We didn't agree, but he'd gotten us in another one of his bets, so he was gettin' more of the fish. We didn't argue with that, even if we didn't agree. When we got to his house, it seemed like the whole neighborhood was standin' in his neighbor's yard. We knew that meant nothin' good. We put all the fish at Caleb's and headed to the neighbor's. They was new in town. Someone's cousins moved down from Georgia somewhere. I don't think anything could've prepared us for what we saw on that porch. The daughter of the house was just a little thing at the time—maybe nine or ten years old. She was just a sittin' on the porch floor all cut up on her legs, arms, and face. Her dress was dirty, torn, and bloody. Her mama was cryin', and she was starin' at the ground like she couldn't hear nothin'. Ricky asked Goodwin what happened and found out Olmos had been rentin' a place out to some guy came down from up north. Said he was here to fish. He attacked the girl that mornin' as she was comin' back from Goodwin's. All the little kids liked to go to Goodwin's. His mama lived out back and gave out candy. On her way home, the girl tripped and fell. She'd been sittin' along the road cryin' cuz when she fell the candy got stuck in her hair. She was afraid her mama would be pretty mad at her for messin' up her hair like that. That New Yorker came and offered to help her get the candy outta her hair and get her cleaned up. Goodwin figured he'd been waitin' for one of those girls to walk on by when no one was lookin'. Took it personal, like a insult on him and his mama. Someone yelled out in the crowd: "There ain't no one gettin' away with this in my town" and the murmur of the crowd agreed. Goodwin nodded his head. No one had seen the guy leave town. Back then there weren't many roads headin' outta town, so it hadn't taken much to be sure he wasn't on the road and weren't no trains leaven' the area just then, so we knew we had him. He had to be in the woods. That was his mistake. We knew the woods better'n he did. He shoulda known better than to mess with Levy boys. We'd get him alright.

Everyone knew then that Miller and Parker had the best huntin' dogs in the area. Usually seemed unfair, cuz they could poach with no law to worry 'bout, but that day we was huntin' a man and we wanted to nab him fast, before he could hurt another little girl. Mostly those dogs tracked deer and hogs, but Miller figured it was a hog we was after and his dogs were good at findin' hogs. They'd find that son of a bitch. We all started over to the shack the guy'd been rentin', and Olmos went in and got some of his clothes for the dogs to scent offa. Those dogs picked up that scent right off. They took off inta the woods on his trail, and all of the men in town took off after 'em. The boys and I didn't have nothin' with us but our knifes. We coulda done the deed with our knifes, but there were so many around us in that group, we knew we was only there as back up.

We followed Miller and Parker and their dogs inta the woods. I swear them dogs had that man treed in five minutes. Like I said, son of a bitch never shoulda run off inta the woods to hide from us Levy boys. We had him treed and surrounded, and he was just cryin' and cryin' like a child, pleadin' for his life. Made all sorts'a claims. Said he worked for the Feds. Said he had money and could pay us all off. We didn't want money. We were there for God's justice. He knew he wasn't gettin' outta there, but every man has a instinct to live. It's natural, and it's somethin' your daddy and I saw over and over again in the war. But this guy—he was goin' down like the rabid dog that he was.

Once we had 'em surrounded, Goodwin took control of the situation while Parker and Miller kept their dogs on him so he wouldn't go nowhere. You could barely hear Goodwin over the dogs barkin' and that man yellin' in the tree. From where I stood, I could see some of the girl's blood on his pants, and yet he was up there yellin' that he didn't do nothin' wrong. He hadn't hurt her none, and she'd liked it. She'd thank him for what he'd taught her. Well, that was 'bout the worst thing he coulda said to that crowd, all surrounded like he was. I can still hear Goodwin in my memory yellin' ta calm the crowd. He told us men, "Listen, y'all. We all know he's not walkin' outta these here woods. We've all got ideas as to how he should end up six feet under." You shoulda heard how the crowd yelled at that. Well, you're a young lady, so maybe you shouldn't, but I got my reasons for tellin' this tale. Anyways, they all had things in mind to do to that man. Goodwin went on to point out that Gavriel was the one whose daughter we was revengin', so it should be up to him how this man went inta the grave. Gavriel, he was angry, but it was a anger controlled by the knowledge that he was not alone in his anger and he was gettin' his vengeance right then and there. As the treed man yelled desperately, alternatin' from pleadin' for his life to tales of how he'd ruined her for all men, Gavriel calmly and quietly said "I don't wanna make killers outta none of ya'll, but I also don't wanna take this piece of shit to the law, exceptin' for ya'll," as he nodded at Miller and Parker who nodded in return, holdin' their dogs and their rifles. "I don't wanna put my daughter through havin' ta talk to no lawmen. The way I see it is no one of us should have this man's blood on our hands, so let's get him down from that there tree and let's all have a shot at him. No one take a kill shot. Let's just all hit him with a bullet each, but not nowhere vital like."

Course, not all of us had guns with us. So Gavriel, he decided we'd all take turns with the guns, all shootin' some where he might survive. "No head shots, no heart shots" until we was sure he was good and dead. Under the cover of about ten guns, me and Ricky climbed that tree and pushed him down to the ground. I think at that point he knew he was done for. He gave up pleadin' and was just cryin'. The men waited 'til we was outta the tree and then Gavriel took the first shot, shooting at the part of the man that had done the most damage, and then all of us took a shot all at once for those who had guns. After that round, Ricky's dad gave his gun to Ricky and I got mine from my daddy, Caleb got his from Goodwin. All of us who hadn't shot yet took a shot. I suppose we could've knifed him, but he didn't seem worthy of gettin' his filth on our knifes.

When it was done, Ricky ran back to his dad's and got a shovel, which none of us had thought to bring. The women saw him comin' for the shovel, he told me later. He nodded at them and Gavriel's wife started cryin' again, others joined her and shouted "hallelujah" or "thank you, Jesus." That was a battle where we knew Jesus was on our side. That man needed to go. Caleb, Ricky, and me was tasked with diggin' a hole as we was the youngest in the crowd. One of the men went and collected lye from the women folk. There wouldn't be much soap makin' that year. Miller and Parker watched to make sure the hole was deep enough, and when it met with their approval, Gavriel and Ricky's daddy pushed that corpse inta the hole and covered it with all the lye that had been gathered. They said it would help the body to decompose faster. Maybe even help with the smell. We all worked to fill the hole back in.

We was all used to coverin' up our tracks from Miller and Parker when we was huntin' outta season, so t'weren't nothin' ta cover up the evidence that we had all been there. When we was done, Miller looked at us boys and said, "boys, go getcha a gator or a deer. Bring it here. Don't need to be too big. Leave the body here, or at least the head," with a wink. Told us the rottin' animal scent would help to cover the body smell, if they were called on to use the dogs to check the area for bodies later. While we was doin' that, Olmos had a bonfire at his place, and he burned everything that man owned. By the time that was done, the ladies in town had brought the girl 'round a bit. Her hair had been cut inta a bob, she'd been bathed and scrubbed and was sleepin' in her mama's arms on the porch. Caleb told me later that she slept in her mama's arms for years after. She became the heart of the town after that, but mostly she became your daddy's heart. This, Anne, is your mama's story, and it was what brought your parents together. Mil was always soft. He wasn't meant to deal out justice to men. He saw your mama hurtin' and that whole day he stayed on the porch with the women. Said he was keepin' 'em safe in case that man snuck on back. But I knew that weren't the truth. He figured sittin' with someone who was hurtin' was the best thing he could do with his time. From that day on, he was determined to help your mama heal, though none of us knew right well how to do that. He thought with his heart, your daddy. Just couldn't take what had happened to your mama. I suppose this explains why your mama was always so protective of you. Why she didn't let you run around with any of the older guys, why she was so picky 'bout who came a visitin' you. Especially when we was in that camp.

We didn't think anyone would come lookin' for that piece of trash, but sure enough, someone did a few weeks later. Turns out he was tellin' the truth when he said he worked for the Feds. Well, he was some sorta politician in New York. He had told his people he was gonna spend a few months fishin' in the Suwannee. He'd heard 'bout the river in that song, I guess, and told his family he would be stayin' near the river in Chiefland. Eventually, when he didn't come back, the Feds were called in. Guess he was workin' on some big law up north, and folks'd figured he'd been taken out by one of his opponents. The Feds came through askin' 'bout him. Not one person they spoke with remembered seein' him. "T'weren't no Yankee stayin' here. I'd remember that," they'd say. Goodwin pointed them in the direction of Miller and Parker, as they was the only local law. As his last known whereabouts was Chiefland, 'corrding to his family, they insisted on takin' Miller and Parker's dogs out to check the local woods, case of a huntin' accident, they said. Guess it never occurred to them that Miller and Parker might be in on the disappearance of their man. Just like Miller and Parker said would happen, the dogs scented to the rottin' gator meat near where we'd buried the body, and with that Miller and Parker were able to cover for the dogs scentin' on the buried body. Feds never suspected nothin'.

Miller and Parker told 'em Dixie County was a better place for fishin' on the Suwannee. Said he probably got one look at Chiefland and moved himself on up to Dixie. Now the rumors of Dixie County had been told these men before they left Gainesville. They'd heard a man could get strung up in Dixie just for bein' a Yankee, so they decided to move on to Lake City, said it seemed like a more likely place for him to have gone. And that was the last time we heard the man's name. We all agreed we'd never speak his name again.

CHAPTER FIVE

School and Church

I suppose I oughta tell ya a little 'bout our school days. Can't have ya thinkin' we was always wild. Of course, for school days we need to back up a spell. We stopped goin' ta school when we was twelve. Had to help daddy with turpentine farmin'. Figured that was the way to money more than books.

While we was in school, we walked inta town every mornin' 'fore the school bell rang. Course, we walked everywhere then so it didn't bother us none. It was one of them one room schoolhouses, but it had plenty a space, not like the school for black kids. The state didn't provide them with a teacher, so they had to raise themselves up one. Didn't seem right, even at the time. Man can't set himself up in life without a education. But what do I know? Never amounted to much myself.

The state sent us Mr. Halal. No one could understand where he got himself a name like that. Heard his mama was Greek, had married some foreigner before migratin' ta Tampa. Others figured he came from up north somewhere. He always looked sorta chiseled in the jaw, and his blue eyes piercin' out from under black eyebrows always gave me the idea he was one of them Greek statues. Girls never stopped talkin' 'bout him. Anyways, I suppose his name, and the mystery 'round it, kept him on the outside. Folks were always suspicious of a newcomer, but he did right by us. Taught us to read and write. Taught some of us Latin. I just learned enough to get myself inta trouble, but Ricky and Mil really studied it. I knew I'd be a farmer or a fisherman, so I didn't take much stock in school. I was the worst, admittedly. Mil liked school. If your daddy had had a opportunity for more schoolin', he woulda taken it.

One year we studied poets and Mil, well he always liked poetry, but I didn't, until we read this one by Donne called "The Flea." Don't think our parents would have liked it none, but most of them couldn't read. I figured out that poem was about sex, well, honestly, Mil explained it to me. Think that's the only poem I remember from our school days. Not sure what possessed Halal to teach us that one, but I'm sure he regretted it. For the rest of that year, and much of the next, I made him pay. Every time he asked a question, I answered with "John Donne" or "The Flea." Halal would ask somethin' like "Who was the King of England during the Revolutionary War?" And I would answer, "John Donne."

"Who is the current US president?"

"John Donne."

"Who wrote *Frankenstein?*"

"John Donne."

"What was the name of Shakespeare's first play?"

"The Flea."

Halal would get so mad. His face would turn all red, and he'd slam a desk drawer sometimes. I can still see the anger lightenin' up his eyes. Ricky always told me I should take my education seriously, but havin' a education didn't help Ricky none in the end.

Caleb was usually my partner in crime. We came up with these words that sounded like curse words. Caleb was the best at it. Halal had made these huge wooden boards, just about as long as my arm; we had to take 'em with us if we stepped out to use the outhouse. Well, the floors in the school-house was wooden, as was all of our floors at the time. Halal, he kept the room quiet. One day, he had the school all testin' or readin'. Everyone was quiet. Caleb, he got himself up and took that wooden pass to go to the outhouse and just as he walked by, he winked at me, so I knew he was up to somethin'. Well, right when he passed one of the pretty girls in school, he started droppin' that pass like it was some kinda hot potato. It clattered on the floor and bounced all the way to the door. It made so much noise, and Caleb yelled out "Oh, ship," just like we practiced. All the kids laughed, but Halal was so mad, don't know how that man put up with us. And yet, I think he liked us. Times was tough then, and Halal, he came from money. Every year he was there, he'd bring a big bird from the city for us for Christmas. Made an excuse that my mama cooked it just the way he liked it. Boy, did she like hearin' that. She'd work hard at cookin' the bird as if she was makin' a feast for a king. She'd be up all night workin' on it, and really, she started days before hand. She'd be in the kitchen all day every day that week, makin' side dishes and pies. Don't think she took off that blue apron all week, and don't rightly know how much she slept. It was the only time we had store bought meat, and it was so good—worth all'a her efforts. Halal was what Mil probably shoulda become, if'n the war hadn't happened. Mil always was the compassionate one. He made us better for knowin' him, like Halal did.

CHAPTER SIX

Bad Boyz

There was these boys in school—Lonny and Nate. Boy was they ugly, all pock marked in the face and dirty all the time. We was poor, but we was always clean when we went out. Mama saw to that. She always said just cuz we was poor didn't mean we could be dirty. God provided water in the river and a comb in the house. We was to be clean at school. I guess Lonny and Nate didn't have a mama that thought that way.

Lonny and Nate was always pickin' on other kids, but especially Jeffrey. His Mama was your neighbor when you was a little thing. Jeffrey weren't born right. Always walked with a limp. He was weak, and he coughed a lot. I think we all knew he wasn't long for this world. He couldn't keep up with us most days, and some days he couldn't even make it to school, especially if it was cold out. On the days he was there, he wanted to eat lunch with us, even though we was several years older. Kids would spread out in the school yard, settin' down in groups and eatin' the lunches their mamas had packed in pails from home. Mil would always make sure we included Jeffrey in our group. One of those days, Lonny and Nate keyed right in on Jeffrey and started tauntin' him, imitating the way he limped and callin' him a mama's boy.

When Jeffrey got nervous, he stuttered, well that just got Lonny and Nate goin' even more. They started laughin' and imitatin' his stutter. Mil wouldn't have that. He ran in there and started poundin' on Nate, who was the bigger of the two. Got that guy square on the jaw and knocked him clear to the ground. Didn't stop there, neither, he jumped on Nate and was wailin' on his face. Caleb, Ricky and I, we had to act. We was blood, and you can't leave your kin alone in a fight. Nate and Lonny was big, but they were no match for the four of us. When we was done, I looked up and Halal was watchin' with a grin on his face. He just looked at me, nodded, and went back inside the school without sayin' a thing. Lunch was a bit longer that day, gave us time to wash up and time for Nate and Lonny to head home. Nate and Lonny changed after that. They was still mean, but they didn't pick on Jeffrey again. In fact, they didn't pick on anyone when the four of us was around.

Jeffrey only lived a couple more years after that. The flu took 'em in the end. Did that to a lot of folks. Nate got more than was comin' to 'em. He was so eager to fight a real bad guy, he volunteered to be the first to go to the Great War. The Germans caught him near Belgium. Impaled him on a pitchfork and left him for the birds. Lonny, he was one of the last to come home, even after your daddy. He was in Belleau Wood. He came out even meaner than he went in. We all get it in the end, I guess. Didn't seem fair, though, even for Nate and Lonny.

CHAPTER SEVEN

Picnics and Such

Mostly, we just saw the other kids in town at school or church. Of course, we was always with Ricky and Caleb, but all the kids were together at church. Every spring the church had a picnic, and pretty near all the town would go, even the Catholics. For a town that didn't have much, folks sure did lay out a spread for a picnic. Ladies was bakin' fruit pies for days and frying up their best chickens. Men was smokin' hogs. Goodwin brought in a big pot of beans from his place. Took real pride in makin' the best batch of beans in the county. The Carusos had cattle, so they brought in a big mess of cream to go with the pies. Most of us couldn't spare cream, if we had any. Ricky had family in Georgia, and they grew peaches, so his mama always brought the best peach pies around. I preferred cobbler myself. My mama, your grandma, made the best peach cobbler, even if the peaches were local peaches.

Anyways, when we was younger, we would get some food—me, Mil, Ricky, Caleb and sometimes Rosie—and we would run for this old cedar tree. It had grown close to the ground, but wide like. The branches were just strong enough to hold our weight. Bein' all spread out like that, the tree was more like a giant bush and it hid us away from all the adults picnicin'. We would each take a fat branch and pretend it was a giant ship and we was goin' out treasure huntin'. Mil was the navigator, and Ricky was the captain. Rosie always wanted captain, but we told her girls can't be captains; that was when we was little guys, things changed as we got older, as they usually do. We sure did have fun. We'd sit there in our branches, eatin' and jokin', and when we was done and our bellies was full, we'd take to our branches and take off, so to speak. We didn't play often, mostly we was out huntin' and fishin', swimmin' or explorin', but that tree brought out the best in us—got us pretendin' and laughin' all day long. Our daddies would have to threatin' the belt to get us out at the end of the day. Don't right know why we didn't go back and play outside of the picnics, but we didn't. Was sorta a ritual for the picnic days, somethin' we looked forward to all year round.

CHAPTER EIGHT

Exploration

Ever since we caught that big gator and had that town-wide BBQ, Goodwin was on our side. Not that we could court his daughter, mind you, but he liked us. I think he wanted to thank us because that BBQ had led to a lot more people in town buyin' food from his place. Well, he was takin' his truck up to St Augustine, up near Jacksonville, to get some coquina rock from a quarry he'd heard of. I guess this stuff had withstood Spanish and British cannons, so he figured it'd be good material for the buildin' he was makin' out back'a his store. Was plannin' on storin' booze in it. He was a future seein' kind of guy, sorta had a intuition 'bout the prohibition that would come later and he didn't plan on followin' no "don't drink booze" sorta laws. His buildin' was gonna withstand anything.

We'd never been over to that side of Florida before, and we'd never seen real waves in the ocean, neither. Well, I think Goodwin knew that. The quarry was on a old Spanish road maybe a mile or two up the road from a beach. First thing Goodwin did was take us four up to the beach. There was no one 'round, so we stripped down to our skivies and took off runnin' for the water. The sand felt like nothin' I'd ever felt before. You never forget the first feel of white sand squeezin' between your toes, pushin' aside all the dirt from the day and fillin' the space with little bits of sand and shells. We didn't mind the pieces of shell diggin' inta our feet none. We was used to runnin' barefoot in the woods, so our feet was tough. Boy, we dove into those waves without a care in the world. We would try to launch ourselves inta the waves so we could sorta sit on the wave as it drove in towards the shore. Ended up tumblin' end over end in the salt water, gettin' sand and salt in every part of our bodies, and we didn't care none. Even managed to catch some dinner in between the swimmin' and the sand buildin'. Boy, your daddy sure could build in the sand. I think it was that imagination of his. He was always makin' stories, and I guess that sorta transferred inta buildin' sandcastles. We'd never even seen a castle or a picture of a castle at that point, so our castles weren't real castles, but they was sorta forts, and since everything was a competition for us boys, we made them to fight each other, see whose castle could hold up to frontal aquatic assaults and the like. Ricky made some sorta launchin' machine. Mil called it a *trebuchet* or some fancy word like that. We played, swam, and fished until long after the sun set.

That night we set up camp on the beach. Goodwin made his bed in the back of his truck, and us guys set up under the stars around a small fire Caleb'd built on the beach. The breeze kept up all night, so the no-see-ums weren't too bad, mosquitos neither. We all slept great, as we always did out on a beach when we was older and would canoe out to barrier islands for the night. In the mornin', we fished for our breakfast. Ricky caught his first shark that day. Caleb cut it up, and Mil and I cooked it. It wasn't too big, but it was big enough to fill us boys and Goodwin, along with some kumquats and bread Mrs. Goodwin had sent. After breakfast, we drove over to the quarry and loaded the back of the truck down with some Coquina for Goodwin's booze cellar. It's funny that us guys helped get those stones, and helped build it, but we never had a drop of alcohol from old Goodwin. He had rules he needed to follow, and rules he didn't mind breakin'. Man was fine with buildin' a still but wouldn't give a couple of youngins a drink.

Once the bed of the truck was full, Goodwin took us back to the beach. He said it was cuz we was all smelly, and he didn't want us stinkin' up his truck on the way back, but I think he knew how much we loved the waves. We'd loaded up the truck in the mornin' and it was afternoon by the time he pulled us outta the water. Caleb and I rode in the back with the stones and Mil and Ricky rode in the truck with Goodwin. Ricky's mama had made Goodwin promise Ricky wouldn't be in the bed of the truck for the long drive. Funny how mamas worry 'bout the little things like truck drives but then send their boys off to wars. Somethin' I never understood.

Anyways, it was late at night by the time the truck got back inta Levy County. For the rest of that summer, we helped Goodwin build his "Fortress of Booze," as he liked to call it, and on the weekends, we went out huntin' and fishin' just us guys, and sometimes Rosie.

CHAPTER NINE

Love and War

The war had been buildin' for a while. Seemed like a grand adventure but one that was far away in places we'd never heard of—so like a adventure we didn't think we'd get to go on. We had to at least look eighteen if we was gonna go, and that took time. We didn't get the paper in town, and none of us but Ricky had a radio in our houses, so sometimes we'd crowd inta Ricky's livin' room and listen to the president give speeches on the state of the nation, or listen to the radio men talk about the state of the war in Europe. Boy, did we wanna piece of that. We kept listenin', all quiet like, until the program was over and the radio started tellin' stories. The only story we was interested in was the news on the war, so we'd switch it off and then go out back'a Ricky's place and talk about what we was gonna do when we got there—how many Huns we was gonna kill. We'd heard they was rapin' women in Belgium and we couldn't let that go. We was gonna go defend women and democracy. Fight to save "King and Country." We was afraid the war would stop before we got there, and talked about tryin' ta lie our way inta servin' overseas in another army or in the Red Cross, at least, but we knew our mamas wouldn't let us go at fifteen or sixteen, so we was gonna have to wait and see if the war was still goin' on when we was old enough. We didn't have no way of shippin' out without our parents' help, and I think Mil and Caleb was against breakin' their mamas' hearts by goin' early. Turns out the war did wait for us, and only some of us had to lie about bein' eighteen when we signed up. Ricky's daddy drove all of us inta Gainesville to sign up. Volunteered as soon as we could, so we was some of the first guys to get shipped off with the U.S. forces. Boy, were our mamas proud when we got in the car to head off to Gainesville. All the daddies woulda gone, but we didn't all fit in the car and the train woulda been too pricey for my daddy and Caleb's daddy, so they sorta formed a crowd around the car, the daddies not goin' and all the mamas. Rosie and your mama was there, too, just as proud as they could be. They all got in their Sunday best to see us off, even Rosie, and that girl did not like dressin' up, well at least not when she was still a youngin. They was all proud of us. Didn't take long to get ourselves signed up. Had to pass a medical exam and such, but that t'weren't nothin' neither, just another ride inta town. Weren't long until we had our date to ship off to boot camp.

It was late spring before it was our turn to go, and the church had one of its big, town-wide picnics planned. We all went, as we always had, but this time we was the guests of honor. We was leavin' not long after, and the church wanted to be a part of the send-off, so to speak, with a service to celebrate. Boy, they made a big service for us, well, bigger than the usual service length, which was already hard for me to stay awake for. Mama used to sit next to me and elbow me to keep me from noddin' off. But that day, I knew I had to keep awake on my own. Wouldn't be right to nod off in the middle of a service in my honor. It was good practice for the military. I knew how to sit through long drawn out speeches when I got there.

Anyways, Kirk, the choir director, led us in the singin'. That day your daddy didn't sing in the choir like he usually did, seein' as how we was the guests of honor. They had this lady singin'. Don't right remember her name. Seems like every church has someone like her. Kind of a nondescript, brown-haired lady. She'd always been singin' at the church, but I do not know why. Must be she was cute when she was little and folks let her think she could sing. Now that she was a grown woman, no one knew how to tell her she shouldn't be a singer. She sang a solo for us that day, takin' from a Cressy poem, somethin' about God help America to help God save the king. Didn't make much sense even then, but it was excitin' despite the notes missed.

After the singin' was done, Pastor David gave a sermon on us being emissaries of God. I'm not sure if that was the case, but it all sounded pretty good. Boy, that pastor could talk. Man droned on sorta monotone like. His words was encouraging and hopeful, but man was it hard to listen as he mumbled on. He had this big, sorta chin, too, seemed to quake when he talked, and on the end of his chin was a mole. Rosie always pointed out the hair growin' outta the mole, but for me it was the movement that kept my eye. The mole kinda bobbed as his chin quivered like a bobber markin' a crab trap in the water. Man like that can't just have a big chin, that would be uneven, so that man had the bushiest eyebrows you ever did see. What a sight. Mama said it wasn't kind to say such things 'bout a preacher, so we mostly said them when she weren't 'round, but that day I was happy for his chin and mole. Watchin' them kept me goin' through the long service.

Well, Ricky, Caleb, and I was all up front in the important chairs behind the pastor and there was this big empty chair next to us for your daddy, but he didn't show. Pastor David preached his whole sermon and no Mil. The guys and I was gettin' pretty fidgety, and not just because the chairs was uncomfortable and itchy, but the whole congregation could clearly see Mil was missin'. We kept lookin' 'round for him, wisperin' 'bout him, but none of us knew where he was. Well, when the pastor finally finished his sermon, he asked everyone to bow their heads and close their eyes, so he could lead us all in prayer. Through his prayer, all we could hear was squeak,

squeak, squeak. Right over that monotone, mumblin' prayer, squeak, squeak, squeak. Mil got himself to the church alright. Right during the closing prayer and sure enough he squeaked his shoes all the way up the aisle of that silent church, passed the pastor, and sat right down next to me. Not sure anyone heard the prayer, so many quiet giggles could be heard over Mil's shoes. Man didn't usually know how to make a entrance, but he sure did that day.

After church the picnic was different than usual. Everything was more patriotic, but more importantly, we was older, and so was the girls. We were spreadin' our blankets on the ground instead of climbin' trees. Seemed like Caleb and me was odd man out mosta the day, but that was alright with me. Sorta liked the excitement and patriotism of the day. Flags was flyin' everywhere, and boy were there pies. I love me a good fruit pie, especially those juicy fruit pies with mixed berries in 'em.

Before we could dig inta the pies, pastor led us all in singin' another round of the song he'd wrote off of'a Cressy poem, after the prayer over the food, that is. We'd already prayed in the church, but preachers always figure you should pray again before eatin'. I wasn't too familiar with Cressy's poems then, but Mil was, and I got one of his books once I got to the front. Anyways, Pastor David led us all in singin' "God Help America to Help God Save the King" again. Not sure why I remember that one, but I can still hear folks singin' it in my head today. Guess I thought of it whole a lot after, when I was stuck in boot camp just a itchin' ta get to the front. Anyways, after the singin' and the prayin', Mil and me, we sat on the blanket your mama had brought. Your mama lay there with her brown hair all laid out on the blanket, not like other girls who liked to keep their hair up at that age. She was distraught over Mil going to war. They'd been visitin' each other for about a year. Folks expected a weddin' announcement any day. He was her greatest comfort and joy, and the only person she wanted to spend time with. I guess that never really changed, even when Mil changed. What I should have realized was that she was his compass. She kept him grounded, and she guided him. Without her, he went astray. But then, on that day, I knew very little about life, least of all about women. I was, after all, there with your daddy and mama and no girl of my own. Your mama, it turns out, was the reason your daddy was late to our sendin' out service at church. He went to help her pack up her picnic food and blanket and lost track of time. They often lost track of time, and everyone else around 'em, and that day was no exception.

Ricky was seated away from us that year. That's what women do to men—drive us apart. He and Rosie had their own blanket spread behind the old cedar tree we used to climb and play ship in. Rosie's blanket was some big ol' red thing her grandma had brought when they moved to the States from wherever they had come from. Not sure how she ended up in Florida, same as everyone else I suppose. She called that blanket a courtin' blanket, said her mama took it with her for every picnic she went on with Rosie and Caleb's daddy. I called it a big, red, itchy thing. I guess that's why it was a courtin' blanket. Weren't much'a anything happenin' on that blanket. It was too itchy. Anyways, her mama'd passed away from pneumonia about two years before that, so the blanket meant more to Rosie than it had before. Her mama wasn't there to see her bein' courted by Ricky, in fact, no one was there to keep an eye on 'em. Her daddy was too blind from grief, even then.

At the end of the church picnic, your mama told your grandma she was stayin' at Rosie's that night, and Rosie told her daddy she was spendin' the night at your mama's. Rosie's daddy didn't talk to people from town anymore, and he didn't come to no picnics, so there was little chance of them bein' caught. So, we all packed up after the picnicin' and met up just outside of town. Ricky came with his daddy's car, and me, your mama, Mil, Caleb and Rosie all filled in and headed down to Cedar Key. Cedar Key was always Mil and me's favorite part of the county. We loved to fish and canoe down there, and this time we was bringin' the girls.

Weather was warm that night, so we kept the car windows down. Caleb had brought some wine he thought his dad wouldn't miss. Man musta had a heck of a lotta wine not to notice a bottle or three missin', but I heard from Ricky the man had a collection of alcohol. Made trips a few times a year to bring home a stash. My daddy was glad to have one big bottle of shine at a time, so he woulda noticed it missin'.

Well, we took those bottles, and we all sang and drank our way to Cedar Key. Took us almost two hours, but it was worth seein' the sunset over the ocean. The bridge goin' inta town goes over a estuary where the Suwannee meets the Atlantic.

There used to be great oyster harvestin' in there, but it had been over harvested a few years before and now there was just enough for those of us who knew where to look. There was still lots of beautiful shoals, though, and there was little patches of green grass on tiny, isolated islands all surrounding the bigger island of Cedar Key. Sorta a collection of islands off the coast.

There was just one police officer on the island and he knew our names, even though we lived so far out. His name was Gentian—another one of them Greeks from Tampa lookin' for space. Boy was he a stickler for speed. Weren't many cars on the island then, so he figured all those cars should be goin' the speed limit, especially those who didn't live on the island. We always slowed down when we crossed the bridge, but not that time. We knew Gentian was already done for the day at five, so we sped on over to the dock where Ricky's family stored canoes at the local marina. The speed made your mama and Rosie laugh, although I suppose the wine was already playin' its part by then.

The water in Cedar Key can be a bit muddy when the tide is out, and that day was no different. The water was way out, and we was gonna have to wade through the muck to get the canoes out to the water. Course we didn't mind none, but the ladies couldn't do that in skirts. Your mama and Rosie had both borrowed a pair of Caleb's pants for that purpose, and they went off behind the car and changed. We all hiked up our pants above the knee and waded through the oozy mud out inta the water. Mud kinda squeezed its way between my toes, and every now and then I'd step on a sharp shell from one'a the oysters that was still lingerin' 'round, for those who knew where to look. Woulda been better if the survivin' oysters didn't congregate where we had to walk but didn't matter none. We was goin' out for a nighttime canoe and the water was perfect for it. Mil and I was carryin' a canoe, and he was so busy laughin' at your mama tip toein' through the mud that he wasn't much help with the weight of the canoe. Once we was out inta the water and past enough of the mud, we all put the canoes down and worked on gettin' in, which is harder after some wine. Caleb and Ricky flipped their canoe twice while gettin' in. Rosie's pants and shirt was soaked through and clinging to her tiny frame, but she just kept on laughin' like she didn't have a care in the world. Your daddy, he was always a gentleman. He held the canoe straight and helped your mama in as if she was the Queen of England. Us guys paddled our way out in the clear, dark night. There was just enough moonlight to see the way directly across from Cedar Key towards Atsena Oti, the smaller island directly across from Cedar Key. Halal told us Atsena Oti meant Cedar Key in the language of the Indians used to live here. So it was Cedar Key off of Cedar Key. Always made me laugh. There used to be a pencil factory on Atsena, but that was back before the hurricanes hit. We guided ourselves to the left of Atsena, since there was still people livin' on the island and we didn't wanna share our last night together with a bunch of strangers. Otherwise we woulda liked to camp and fish there. Anyways, the graveyard on Oti wasn't too romantic, and there was another island past Atsena—that was where we wanted to fish and camp with the girls. The island was empty that night, like it always was. Just us and some shore birds. It was a nameless and narrow island, small enough that we could walk around it, if the roughness of the broken shells on shore didn't stop us. We pulled inta the right side on to the white sands past the shells and went right towards the palm tree that had fallen in last year's storms.

Caleb and me set up a nice fire for the girls. We'd brought some hog meat from home to cook over the fire, and the girls had brought some things to go with the meat. They was always good like that. Made me always glad to have them 'round. Even if I didn't have a girl of my own, I got the benefits of your daddy and Ricky courtin' girls, since they always brought enough food for the lot of us. Your mama had made some corn bread and potato salad. Come to think of it, my canoe had carried the firewood and food; there wasn't a lot of good fuel on the island, so we'd brought it in. That might have been the reason our canoe didn't get tipped more than your mama bein' on the canoe, that and her corn bread was nothin' we was gonna risk fallin' in the salty water. Your mama was like a sister to me, and I didn't mind dunkin' her none. I did mind wet firewood and salty, wet food. Well, anyways, Caleb and I had a fire goin' right quick and we was slow cookin' the meat over the fire. Mil took your mama off on a walk to the other side of the island. They took the path to the south towards Cedar Key, and Ricky and Rosie took the northern path away from the island, which was a bit more rocky and slow goin'.

That's how it was in those days, me and Caleb sittin' alone while the four of them went off. But like I said before, your daddy was always a gentleman. The guys in his unit teased him for that when he was in the war. He'd gone off to ask your mama to marry him that night. Wanted to ask her when they was alone, but when they got to the spot he'd picked out, they found a dead sea turtle. Must've washed up in the tide. That sort of thing didn't bother me and Mil none, but your mama always loved turtles. She wanted Mil to save it, but it was long past savin'. She insisted Mil give it a right proper burial, and he did. Your mama had a way of gettin' what she wanted from your daddy, and that turtle was no exception. He told me later he used a stiff piece of tide wood to dig a hole in the sand and push the thing inta the hole. It was a big ol' thing. Probably died of old age, givin' its size. Since there weren't a lot of sand or dirt to build a mound over the thing, all stickin' outta the hole like it was, he pulled a smaller downed palm tree on top of the grave and your mama made a burial marker outta the brush nearby and some seashells. Figured it would be safe there, and if she was happy, Mil was happy. After the burial, she insisted he say a few words over the grave, like in a normal burial service. He told me he quoted Walt Whitman's "O Captain! My Captain!" and she liked that. Buryin' a smelly, old turtle sorta killed the romance for right then, so they headed back to the fire with me and Caleb. We had just finished cookin' some meat, so we all sat down and started diggin' in, them on their blanket, and Caleb and I on the other side of the fire, talkin' 'bout the comin' war and all the things we was gonna do when we got there.

Rosie and Ricky were gone a bit longer. You see, Rosie couldn't swim. Really bothered her when we was kids and we'd swim without her. Lots of girls couldn't swim back then. I guess folks didn't think swimmin' was lady like, but it wasn't like that with Rosie and Caleb's parents. Rosie was always out in the woods with us by then. She could hunt and fish and skin a squirrel just as good as I could, or almost as good. She just never learned to swim, and since she could do most things we could do, we wasn't in a hurry to teach her how to swim. Sorta held it over her head when we was younger that we could do somethin' she couldn't. The summer before, Rosie had come on one of our campin' trips. Your mama wasn't allowed on overnight campin' trips, but Rosie got to come. Her daddy figured Caleb would look out for her reputation, but she was always Ricky's girl, and everyone respected that. Well, on that earlier trip us guys decided to swim across the Suwannee, where we was campin' at the time, and then swim right back to the side of the river our camp was set up on. That way, we could see who was the fastest swimmer. All the guys in Chiefland did that. Some never made it back, and we found their bodies a few weeks later, but Ricky and Caleb and I knew we could do it, so it was a matter of who could do it faster. It was never much of a contest. As with most things, Ricky was always first place, and Caleb, Mil and I fought for second place. We fought dirty, too. That night Caleb got me thinkin' a gator was headed for Mil to slow me down enough so he could win. Worked. Now Rosie, she sat as judge, but she was pretty put out that night. She hated that we could all swim and she couldn't. She'd had it. Made Ricky promise he would teach her and that night in 1917, before we went off to war, he promised to take her to the other side of the island and teach her. Not sure if he taught her or not. Never asked. They was awful happy when they came back to the fire, and she never mentioned if she could swim or not after that night. There were lots of things she didn't mention. I didn't find out she was expectin' until I got home from the war and she had Ricky's baby sittin' with her. She intended on not tellin' Ricky, too. Didn't want him worryin' while he was fightin' for the country, but in the end, she did write to him and tell him just before the baby was born. Didn't want no one else tellin' him. Boy, she was the talk of the town, so it was likely someone woulda told Ricky. Not many girls had babies on their own then. Usually went off to a aunt's up north and came back with no baby. Not Rosie. She's always been strong and self-reliant like. She knew she'd be okay, but then again, she always figured Ricky was comin' home to raise his son.

Well, once Rosie and Ricky came back that night, they joined us 'round the fire and we all ate. Rosie had brought some cake which had gotten a bit soggy, but we ate it anyways, 'long with another bottle of wine Ricky hadn't mentioned he had earlier. We sat there after dinner and we all sang and laughed for hours. We didn't drink much back then, so the bottles of wine was all we had that night, and even that much was unusual for us. Levy county was a dry county long before the nation got the notion to go dry. We didn't need it much then, neither, if you can imagine me and your daddy feelin' that way. We just sat with our friends and sang and ate and it was enough. We stayed there together until the sun came up. We watched it raise itself up over the ocean, and once it did, your daddy got down on one knee and asked your mama to marry him that day. We were all shippin' off to bootcamp that evenin', and he couldn't stand leavin' unless he knew your mama was officially his. Of course, she said yes. We all knew she would. After that we all packed up and rowed ourselves home with no tippin' this time. Didn't want the girls havin' ta explain why they was wet.

We went straight to your mee-maw and papa's house, and your daddy asked if they'd care to come out to the weddin'. Of course, they did. Your daddy had told them ahead of time he'd be askin'. He'd asked your papa for her hand in marriage, he just hadn't told the man that we'd all be overnight on an island. Boy did your mee-maw fuss over your mama that day. Did her hair right pretty with flowers from her garden and put your mama in her own weddin' dress she'd saved in a trunk and been secretly gettin' ready for this day. We all walked to the courthouse from there. My daddy and mama came and met us there. Mil had it all planned out. Judge done married them before noon and we all shipped out at six. They had a five-hour honeymoon, and not a reception or party after to speak of, though mama made a bit of somethin' for us. We still had packin' ta do, not that we had much to pack. Anyways, we'd been up the whole night before, so we wanted sleep more than we wanted food, so we ate some food on the train that the girls had packed for us and then we slept the entire ride, all four of us sittin' together. That was the beginnin' of the Great War for us, though I don't think there was anything great about it.

We had joined early. Didn't want to wait 'til we was forced, and we all wanted to go together. Truth be told, we was excited to do our part. The word was President Wilson was goin' ta call up a army, and we figured if we volunteered, we'd be sure of gettin' there 'fore the fightin' lolled. Mil was just willin' ta do what we wanted to do. He thought war would be an adventure. We all did. Thought he'd get somethin' ta write about; in the end, I guess a lot of guys did get somethin' ta write about from that war, but not your daddy. Because we were early volunteers, there was no units from Florida for us to train with yet, so they shipped us out of state by train.

Trainin' in boot camp was pretty short then. Most of the guys had never held a gun. City boys. I think that was why we was put in that unit. All those city boys left college to join, but with all their learnin' they didn't know how to fire a gun, or how to find their way in the woods, and they'd never killed a man. Guess the powers that be figured us Levy boys would lead the way, but mostly in boot camp we just made fun of the other guys for not knowin' things like the difference from regular ivy and poison ivy, and they made fun of us for the way we talked. That's alright. We didn't never flag no man on a gun range, so we figured we would still be better than those guys and should help 'em not to get themselves or someone else killed as a result of their own stupidity.

The gun range was where we focused mostly. We'd always

thought Ricky was the sharp- shooter and we was just average, but the four of us was the best shooters on base by far. They put us in charge of trainin' a group of the guys in the off-hours. Wasn't so easy to do as there was only one gun for every five guys. The rest all practiced with wooden guns. Didn't do them much good in the end, but we did what we could, until the ammunition ran out, which it always did.

One day we was havin' the guys take their turns firin' the guns at the range, the rest of the guys was practicin' with their wooden guns, when Mil came runnin' out yellin' for the firin' ta stop. He swore there was a turtle on the firin' range, a big one. Well Ricky called for the firin' ta stop, as he was leadin' practice that day. We all went out there to save Mil's turtle, and don't you know it was just a rock? Boy, Mil never heard the end of that and much of the ribbin' came from the three of us. Didn't let other guys laugh at my brother. That was my job. I reckon he saw what he thought was a turtle and thought of your mama. She always did love savin' turtles. The guys all called your daddy Turtle Man for years after that. Some of 'em probably didn't even know why, but once a nickname starts, you're stuck with it.

Anyways, most days on the firin' range weren't funny. Not sure what the point of those wooden guns even was. What can a man learn about war from holdin' a toy gun like a little boy? Well, we tried to at least practice not pointin' in the wrong direction, and how to load fast when there were real guns to practice with. Figured it was important to load quickly so as to fight off as many Huns as possible. We'd start trainin' with loadin' over and over, and then we'd move on to actual firin' of the gun. That helped with makin' sure they remembered not to flag the gun before they had one that could fire. They was always impressed with how well the four of us guys could shoot. Set up competitions to see which of us was best, which ended when they realized it was always Ricky. It was fun, though, at night, to have a bit of competition. The officers had to limit us cuz of how low ammunition stock was. I think they wanted to see what we could do, too. I almost took Ricky once, but it was like he had some sorta spiritual connection with the gun. He could make it do things I couldn't. Even as I got better, so did he. I wasn't never gonna take that guy.

It was about that time that I was separated from the rest of the guys. Turns out some fella from the Carolinas had come in with influenza. It was just startin' then, and cases weren't noticed until early 1918, but this guy had it none the less. Seein' how it had just got started, the Army wasn't good at catchin' symptoms. I had it within a few days of meetin' the guy in the chow hall. I could say I wish I'd never met him, but I suppose, in a way, he saved my life. I got so sick from influenza, I couldn't ship out with the Ricky, Mil, and Caleb. They kept me in the hospital for weeks. Eventually, I overcame, which is more of a chance than many Americans got. I hear tell that over 100,000 Americans died in October of 1918 alone, and it was that same month that my daddy wrote to tell me that mama had lost her fight with influenza. We'd left her only a few months before, and she'd been fine. I knew there was a chance that she could lose me in the war, but it never crossed my mind that I could lose my mama. Course, lots of guys were losin' buddies and sweethearts about that time. Lots of us lost folks. For me, I lost my mama, and I lost the opportunity to serve under Patton on the Western Front. Eventually, I lost my daddy, too. The stress of losin' mama was too much for him. Doc wrote me in Italy and said daddy died of a broken heart, though I expect it had more to do with tryin' ta solve his sorrow with a bottle of moonshine. That sort of runs in the family. No mind. You take what life gives you, and you move forward, and eventually I did. I got my strength back, and I got new shippin' orders.

CHAPTER TEN

Death in the Afternoon

Once I was healthy enough, they shipped me off with the 332nd regiment to Italy. Got there in time to witness the Battle of Vittorio-Veneto, although I suppose that don't mean too much to you. Your mama told me you read a lot, so maybe one day you'll take an interest in old Uncle Will and look it up. The battle went well for the Allies, if you can call the deaths of about 70,000 men in one battle "going well." I looked that up once. That's the amount of soldiers on both sides. I separated enough of the dead in my life. I don't separate 'em no more. The dead are just that—dead. They don't care no more where they got buried or who they got buried next to.

Anyways, the battle was the first I'd seen. I wasn't there to fight. Since I was an American, they sent me and some other guys in American uniform to tour the front and encourage the Italians that more of us was comin'. I don't think it worked. Sometimes, we would parade around different roads outside'a town, then change our uniforms and do it again so as to make the Austrians think there was more of us. It was a humiliating job, just watchin' guys go to battle and not gettin' ta help. Such is the luck of the draw. Eventually, with all my elbow rubbin' in the trenches between fights, I was able to convince them of my sharpshootin' skills and they reacquisitioned me. I was a pretty good shot next to most guys. That was the first thing I talked to Hemingway about. Both of us were stuck watchin', and both of us knew our way 'round a rifle. When I was allowed to go forward as a sharpshooter, I looked for him to see if he could be sent up with me, but I heard he was sent back to Milan for jaundice or somethin' like that. Probably wouldn't'a let him go, anyways. But we can talk more about Hemingway later. While he was off at the hospital in Milan, I got to take part in the last few days of the battle; I was pretty far from the front lines, but that's kinda a braggin' point for sharp shooters. I may not have been in the trenches like your daddy, but boy I got to take some Krauts out with my rifle. I sat up in my spot in between two rocks in a hill over lookin' the action and just pecked 'em off. Aimed for officers first. Those bastards just sendin' men to their deaths. I got a few of 'em. Guess that battle makes me one of the fortunate sons.

Or maybe the war does seein' as there was over 300,000 American lives lost in this war. They said the deaths overall in the war was so high, the world would learn and there'd never be another war like it, but you and me know that weren't true.

After the battle was over, the Wops had the Austrians on the run, and I was along for the ride. We chased 'em down the mountains and past the Piave and eventually the Isonzo in Gorizia. I went all the way with the guys inta what had been Austria. Some place called the Bainsizza Plateau. Boy, the landscape was amazing. Not like anything I'd see growin' up as a Florida boy. The mountains run like a spine just north of the plain and there was a bit of snow on the top of 'em, but the fields in between was still green. This was farmin' land much like home, but all the fields was empty from the war. The white plaster houses in the villages was broken, and the people were hidin' in Italy. I never understood why they fled to Italy, seein' how Italy was the one invadin', but the further I went inta Austria and saw the destruction, the more I understood. The area was destroyed, and the only options left for survival was fleein' ta Italy or movin' ta a camp run by Austrians. Don't no one want to be in a camp.

When the war was over, we was stuck digging up those left behind. Americans weren't doin' this in Italy; mostly they was movin' the dead in France, but since I'd got myself attached to a Italian regiment, I was stuck doin' what they was doin' til someone higher up remembered I was there and moved me.

On the weekends, or whatever days we managed to get off, we would walk, crowd inta a car with a officer, or take trains to other parts of the front. I was ready to get home to the Suwannee, and I had already determined this was my last time outta my own country. I wanted to be where everyone speaks my language, so I figured while I was there, I would take every chance I could get to explore the areas 'round me, now that the fightin' was done. Plus, the ladies always liked to hear the way I talked, even if they couldn't understand me none. They liked to see my gator claw hangin' 'round my neck, too. Thought I was some sorta savage. Made me laugh when they weren't 'round. Mil, Caleb, Ricky and I had to convince the brass to let us wear those claws. Said it was like a icon. Connected us to our saint. Can't remember what Caleb called that saint, but the man signin' our papers and takin' our stuff believed Caleb, so off we went to impress the ladies of Europe with our claws.

Well, when I was out explorin', one time we went to the town of Plezzo. Funny name for a town. It used to be called Bovec, I heard. Not sure which was better. Anyways, funny name but not a funny place. During the Battle of Caporetto, the Germans had dropped gas on the town. Terrible stuff. The town had been emptied of civilians already, so it was all Italian soldiers, and that gas killed all six or seven hundred of those guys before they could even put their gas masks on. All those guys dead in less than a minute. The dead would've been everywhere. In the rush to deal with the dead, they weren't dealt with proper like, or at least that's what the powers that be decided. It was those same powers sent those guys to their deaths, so I'm not sure they's the ones shoulda been makin' the decision. They also weren't the guys that had to do the diggin'. If they was, they probably woulda made a different decision. Anyways, it was much like the area I had been sent to, only prettier. Mountains all around lookin' at ya like "come climb me," but after a week's work, most guys just wanted to drink, same as the way time was spent where I was closer to the Piave river. We spent time explorin', alright, but not out hikin' no mountains. Besides, there was still live ordinances off in those mountains and some of the guys assigned to bring down the dead and the stuff left behind—some of those guys got themselves blown up by steppin' in the wrong spot. Any interest in mountain climbin' went away every time word got out of another guy blowed up.

I suppose if I'd stayed with my unit, this wouldn't'a happened to me, but at that point, I guess someone figured I should stay there still or they forgot me. Weren't so bad, bein' as I had a guy assigned to help me communicate, but I'd never been one of those guys to watch others work, so I always pushed to be involved in what all the others was doin', and this time what they was doin' was diggin' up all the dead. We had to dig 'em up, and sometimes separate them as there'd been no time for separate graves in some places, or sometimes the dead from both sides'd been put together. Can't have that none. Some of the graves'd been blown up, too. So, we dug 'em up, and searched 'em for any identification. They'd all been given these necklace type things that had metal boxes attached and a paper inside with their identification. Trouble was these guys'd been buried in the mud and the dirt. It had rained. The bodies had started to decompose. Some of 'em had been in there for a few years. I'll spare you the details, but it was pretty hard to read what was left'a those papers. Some guys'd been blown to bits, so those necklaces weren't there. Then we'd have to look for pockets that might have letters or such to identify with. I always thought that was tricky, cuz sometimes a fella'd pick up a letter from a fallen friend to deliver. Wasn't no one listenin' ta me, though, no one that mattered. So, we dug 'em up, identified 'em, and buried them in individual marked graves, separate from the Austrians and Germans.

After a day or two of this, I understood why the guys drank so much. The smell never left your mind. Could always remember what an old, dead body smelled like. The guys were willin' ta share their drink; we had wine every night, sometimes cheap wine. I got to where I could tell the cheap stuff from the good stuff pretty quick, but we drank whatever we could. There was always girls that wanted to make friends with soldiers, too. I know you don't wanna hear about all of Uncle Will's adventures in Italy, but I want you to see how it was, how it changed me. I couldn't sleep at night from the dead visitin' me and the smell lingerin' on my hands. The alcohol was free or cheap. It was like that with all us guys in one way or another.

Better'n talkin' about the dead and the drinkin', I did visit more towns on days off, and after seein' all they had to deal with the dead in Plezzo, I learned to avoid the wrong areas on other visits so as I could have some fun and not think about the dead no more. One day we got ourselves to Caporetto itself. That was the scene of Italy's big defeat, lost well over half a million 'tween the dead, the captured, and the injured. Was such a big loss, it became a byword of sorts. Italy's embarrassment and Germany's big win. Well, the village was sorta a resort lookin' village, like a place you might wanna go with a family and play in the river and hike in the mountains. Seemed like it was a place that was meant to be peaceful and welcomin', but it was the center of so much fightin'. I guess that's how it is, though, when one country has somethin' the neighbor country wants, somethin' nice like a little peaceful mountain village.

These towns, Plezzo and Caporetto, didn't want no foreigners like me stayin' in 'em. These were the towns the Italians had been fightin' ta take for the whole war, and they only got the towns in the end because they sided with the Allies in the war at the promise of bein' given the towns after the war. From what I was told and the little I got to see, they was Italianizin' those towns. Forcin' the people to change their names, the town names, and their languages. Got rid of anything that didn't sound and look Italian, even though weren't no Italians livin' there before the war. So mostly, we was supposed to stay in what had been Italy before the war, so we didn't see. But my guys snuck me inta those areas cuz they saw me as their friend, and also cuz they didn't care none what their leaders thought of them now that the war was over. Or at least that's what they said when none of the big guys was around.

When I ran inta Hemingway years later in the Keys, we talked about Italy and what we'd seen there. He told me

Mussolini had the dead dug up a second time. Mussolini had giant ossuaries built all over the old Front and required all the Italians moved to 'em. He didn't know what Mussolini did with the Austrian dead, but the Italians were buried in giant steps by the thousands. Their names were on the walls and the word *"Presente"* was written on the steps as if there was a role call and the dead was answerin' "Present"—ready to serve their fatherland again. I was pretty sure if given the chance all those guys woulda gone back home to their sweethearts and they never woulda gone off to war, but the Italian government thought otherwise. Or at least Mussolini did.

I've gotten off track. I need to tell you a little 'bout your daddy's time in war.

It's a difficult story to tell you 'bout, cuz I wasn't with him to see how it was. Josh wasn't with him, neither. You remember Josh, or at least I hope you do. Well, Josh had wanted to join early on, and he had family in New York, so he went up there, train hoppin' the whole way and joined up. Joined with a cousin, or a second cousin twice removed, or somethin'. Family of some sort. Said they was brothers and lied about his age and his address, not that anyone cared. Ended up in the 369th Infantry Regiment of New York's National Guard. French called 'em the Harlem Hellfighters. It's easier to see Josh as a hell fighter than to imagine someone thinkin' he was from Harlem. Even though he was a black guy, he was far too country to be from Harlem.

I got all of that outta Josh one night sittin' 'round a camp fire, not that it was much. Your daddy's story I pieced together from guys when we was in DC and bits your daddy'd told Josh when we was all livin' together. Josh was the kinda guy that made you feel you could talk to him, and I guess your daddy did. Anyways, they was part of the American Expeditionary Force. We'd joined in March of 1917, and by May, they was there in France. Because Ricky, Caleb, and your daddy knew how to drive, thanks to Ricky's daddy, and of course they was also good shots (which is what made them stand out in trainin', catchin' the eyes of the brass), they was put in Patton's tank corps, the 327th Tank Battalion, to be exact. By August, Pershing had our guys along the Saint-Mihiel Salient, which was a sorta sharp angle in the German line. The Germans had held that ground for three years. They was all trenched in. I don't know how many guys died along that line, but Pershing came in and threw hundreds of thousands more at the line. Worked, too. Tanks like your daddy's ended up leading the way so as to cut the barbed wire and take out machine guns—something Caleb and Ricky was particularly good at, from what I've heard. They went towards a town called Essey and met up with MacArthur. By the time they got to Pannes, paint was flyin' offa the tanks.

After that, 'bout a month later, they was on to the Meuse-Argonne offensive, goin' after the German Second Army. Thought they would end the war; course things don't usually work out the way we think they will. I suppose those battles did help end the war, though. Didn't end up quite how Patton thought it would. Patton thought this would be the biggest battle in the history of the world, but he always was a arrogant bastard.

Gettin' back to your daddy's story, as they moved forward, a fog fell so as they couldn't see in front of themselves. It's funny how weather plays a part in war. Patton took your daddy, Ricky, Caleb, and another guy on foot to spy out ahead instead of hunkerin' down in some place called Chippy. Patton grabbed guys from another unit and had 'em all dig trenches real quick. Rumor has it they weren't diggin' fast enough, so he hit one of the guys on the head with a shovel. Guy never got up again. Let him be buried next to the trench. Well, Patton and his men didn't stay there neither. He rallied 'em to charge up a hill with German machine guns on the top, just ahead of a few tanks, instead of waitin' for back up. The sort of bullshit that made Patton a hero, I suppose. Ricky, Caleb and your daddy went chargin' up with Patton. The guys in DC laughed about it and said your daddy went chargin' up sayin' "this might be the gates of hell, but I won't back down," or somethin' like that. He impressed guys. Stayed in the memories of those who talked behind the lines. When they got to workin' their way up the hill, there never was much of a fight. In a few minutes, all of the one hundred men who went after Patton was dead, except for your daddy and another guy. They was fortunate, they was told. Ricky and Caleb wasn't so fortunate. They was shot down and died almost instantly. Dead and later buried in a foreign country in foreign dirt.

That still didn't stop Patton. He wanted 'em to keep goin' up that hill and inta the German machine gun fire. Fortunately, Patton got shot and your daddy and the other guy saved him and pulled him inta a shell hole for safety. Shoulda let him lie there with all the men he'd led to their deaths. Woulda been better for your daddy and so many others.

An hour or so later, Patton's tanks got there and more followed 'em. That's what you need—tanks—if'n you want to take out German machine guns entrenched on top of a hill you's at the bottom of. The men who came later called that area a cemetery of unburied dead, so many guys died from followin' Patton, and our Ricky and Caleb was there with 'em. Lay'n unburied in French soil. But that's not where your daddy lost his arm.

After the Saint-Mihiel Salient, George Marshal moved your daddy and the guys he was with up to the Meusse-Argonne Offensive. Got to work with the Frenchies then, though I don't know if your daddy liked that bit or not. Never heard him tell otherwise, so I guess he did. Well, this was the largest and deadliest of our involvement in the war, and he was servin' under the frogmen's command, so maybe he didn't like the French none, now that I think about it. He was in the Verdun section, north of the city of Verdun. Your daddy never did have good luck, and bein' there weren't no kinda luck. He stayed there from the end of September all the way through the end of the war and got hisself injured a few weeks before the war ended. He never really talked about this part. He was one of almost 100,000 American guys to get wounded in this offensive, so I suppose there weren't much to talk about that he'd want to be thinkin' bout after the fact. Seems the lateness of his injury was one of the reasons he ended up stuck on the

Front waitin' for transfer back to better hospitals for so long. Maybe that's why his arm got the way it did. He'd been shot in his left arm, but it weren't tended to right at the get go. By the time a better doctor was sent to the front, the guy had to remove a lot of what was left of Mil's left arm. While he was healin' in a hospital, I was already on my way home. The Italians didn't need no Americans seein' the Italinization of the new land they had claimed, so while Uncle Sam may have forgot I was on loan, the Italians eventually did not. I was sent packin' long before your daddy.

CHAPTER ELEVEN

The Return

When I got offa the train back home, there wasn't a victory parade waitin', like in some cities. I guess there weren't enough of us comin' offa trains at one time. It was just me that day. Didn't right know where to go, so I walked home. Found out pretty quick that Olmos didn't want me there. He'd held the house 'til I got back, and he let me know what an inconvenience that was to him. His daddy had fought in the Civil War, he told me, and he couldn't rightly empty the house on me while we was off protectin' democracy. Truth be told, I knew he'd done me quite a favor in holdin' the house for me, but I didn't tell him that. There weren't much to deal with. Daddy's work boots were sitting by the door. Not sure what they buried him in, as those was his only shoes. I suppose they figured I'd need 'em when I got back, and I did. He also left some work clothes, not much more'n a pair of work jeans and two shirts; that was enough for me to look for work in. Mama had her extra dress and her blue apron hangin' in the kitchen. Your mama kept the apron and an older widow in town was thankful for the dress. Aside from that, there were some pots and dishes and such in the kitchen, some pictures and things in the sittin' area, and I gave those to your mama, too. She was still waitin' on your daddy. He was in the hospital healin', only we didn't know that just then. We hadn't heard from him in a bit, and folks kept askin' if we was worried. I'd tell 'em no, but I was. They figured as I was his twin, I had some connection to him and I knew. I didn't. He was all I had left, and I thought he'd come back. That was all. With Caleb and Ricky gone, losin' Mil seemed impossible, as if the world could only do so much damage and the limit had been reached.

That first night home, I didn't go and see anybody. I was tired from the long walk from the train, and I needed time. I knew where daddy had kept his stash. Mama always acted like she didn't know, but if Mil and me knew, so did Mama. Daddy didn't drink often, and mama didn't complain when he did. I put on daddy's work clothes, grabbed his bottle of shine and sat down on the back step. They didn't have much, but they sure did have a view. The area behind mama and daddy's house, along with most of Chiefland, was pretty level. Not many hills like you can find in Williston, but their back step faced west and daddy had cleared the trees between his place and Olmos' farm. The yard was pretty green up top, but the grass was dyin' at the roots. Typical Florida grass, more sand spurs and weeds than grass, but it was pretty as long as you was wearin' shoes. Daddy had left mama's favorite oak tree in the back yard. He said it was for her, but that granddaddy oak weren't goin' nowhere without several men haulin' it out. I suppose mama knew that, too. That tree sprawled to the heavens and several of the branches was thicker than I was, although I suppose that wasn't sayin' much at the time. The Spanish moss made the branches look even thicker, hangin' as it was off the branches like a hoary beard. Lookin' past the tree I could see Olmos' pasture spreadin' out behind the branches. The pasture was a light green fresh with rye, and it was speckled with black heifers. The sun had just started to set when I sat down, and it was spreadin' red and purple across the sky. Sittin' there, sippin' daddy's moonshine, wearin' his jeans and lookin' out at the view he and mama had for years, all felt right with the world. I hadn't been sure before that moment what I would do when I got back, but I knew then I would find work, and I would pay Olmos what he was askin' for havin' kept the house. It just felt right comin' home and sittin' in the quiet. I built myself a little fire that night, and I sat up against the oak tree sippin' daddy's drink and thinkin' most of the night, but eventually the cicadas and the drink put me to sleep. When mornin' came, I got up and went and found myself a job. Folks were happy to see me, for the most part, and it didn't take long for me to find work.

Your daddy weren't as lucky when he came back. Turns out his time in the hospital really stretched out. Some sort of infection, I guess. They didn't give him a mirror for a while, so he didn't know how bad some of his injuries were. He had been in a field hospital at first, and not many letters found their way in or out of the hospitals on the front, and if they did, they got lost somewhere along the line. Transportation was an issue for the guys in his field hospital, so he'd been stuck for a bit without much care. He'd been injured in his left arm, below the elbow, like I said before. He didn't remember much about it. The injury was bad enough, they'd had to amputate just above the elbow. Gave him what he called a nub. He was there a few days too long. The front shifted, as it did sometimes, and while he was bein' transported they fell under a gas attack. Mil hadn't been able to get his mask on fast, bein' new to life with one and a half arms. The guy next to him had put it on for Mil, but the damage was already done. Really, that probably woulda done him in at some point. Mustard gas was like that. Did damage, but the damage didn't stop. Some guys died years later from what that shit had done to 'em. Mil's face took the brunt of it. Stuff hit him and caused his face to get all red and swollen, formed blisters and sores that sorta ate away at the skin. Like the skin just died or melted offa him. I saw guys like that recoverin', but no one I knew had that happen while I was over there. When the sores healed, he was left lookin' like the right side'a his nose had sorta melted down towards his lip and his lip had curled up to meet it. Nurses felt for him, bein' as he was such a handsome guy goin' in. He was worried what your mama would think'a him. For the first time, he wondered if she'd take him back. Course she did, but that's the sorta thing all guys worried about in his situation, and some girls didn't take 'em back. Only took one girl in a hundred to be that bitch and then all the guys worried about their girls back home.

Anyways, the nurses felt for him and they moved him forward to a doctor who knew what he was doin'. Guy tried to put your daddy's face back together, but don't see as it did much good, and it kept him overseas for longer, which left all of us worryin', seein' as he didn't write. When he finally did, he sent the letter to me at your mama's house. Wanted me there when she read about his injuries, figured I would talk her through it. Turns out he didn't need to worry none. She had sat with Rosie cryin' at night enough to know how lucky she was to get her soldier home. We wrote him back that day to tell him how much we both needed him home. Her letter was a bit longer than mine.

When he finally got off that train, all of us was there— me, Rosie, you and your mama and Ricky's parents. Seein' as he'd given us warnin', we knew when to be there. He always thought ahead more'n I did. We just all fell on him, huggin' him and cryin'. It had been too long. We took him out that night, it was a Saturday, so felt like we should be out celebratin' and celebrate we did. Mostly your mama just smiled and shook her head. We had the whole place to ourselves, all closed down for the private party and we sat up inta the night eatin', drinkin' and laughin'. I tried to give your mama and daddy space after that, as much as was possible seein' as I'd been livin' with you and your mama and helpin' you two pay rent and buy food, lookin' over things for your daddy and helpin' ta keep things runnin'. Moved out on my own then and took some time to think on what the next step would be for me, but there weren't much time to think. Seems decisions often get made for us, or at least we think they do.

CHAPTER TWELVE

Dry Run

Each chapter in our lives eventually comes to an end. While I was in the war, I thought it would never end, but it did. There weren't much for me to come home to. Mil had you and your mama, but I had no one. Everything in me had changed. "I became a man" they said, but I was a man when I left—a free man. War didn't make me a man, it made me a changed man.

It was Rosie who got me through the adjustment back home. She'd seen me in church your daddy's first Sunday back. Guess I blended in more when it was just us, sittin' and eatin' together, but in large groups I couldn't hide. Felt I didn't fit in anymore. Couldn't see things the way the rest of the townsfolk saw things. I'd seen too much to think I was some kinda hero or that I had done God's service for him in fightin' the evil Hun. Thoughts kinda bubbled up in me when I got in with the rest of the town and had folks pattin' me on the back, but also tellin' me I needed a shave or now that I was back, I should put the bottle aside. They could smell it on me. I suppose they was lookin' out for my best, or thought they was, but it didn't feel that way at the time.

Anyways, that first time back at church, I was goin' for you and your mama's sake. I'd found reasons to skip church when your daddy wasn't back. I could always work on the house or the yard for your mama while she took you to church. When Mil came back and wanted to go, I knew I had to go, so I did. I hadn't been avoidin' Rosie, but I hadn't found my way to go spend time with her on my own neither. I'd known I should go and see her when I first got home, and the baby, but I couldn't face them. I was ashamed I'd returned and Ricky hadn't. He'd always been a better man than me, and he shoulda been the one to come home. Hell, he had a baby to come home and raise. Figure that while the flu had killed my mama, it had saved me, else I woulda been there with Ricky and Caleb and I wouldn't'a come home without 'em. Not if we'd been together. So, I put off seein' her and I put off goin' ta church as long as I could. Turns out I was goin'ta need her that mornin'. She always seemed to be tuned inta when I would need her ear or her shoulder. She was good like that.

That first Sunday, your mama wanted your daddy and I to go to church with her. She'd worked hard fillin' in at the school with Halal off in the war. Managed to get herself a little house in town for the two of you. Figured I better go along with what your mama wanted, even if once Halal got home, I was helpin' ta pay rent. At the time, the only suit I had was the one I got when I left the war. It was a little worse for the wear, but it was all I had. Your mama walked me and your daddy inta that church just as proud as could be. Struttin' herself like a peacock, she was. You'd think that she was the Queen of Sheba. Not everyone was proud of us as she was. We was a bit hungover from the night before. Mil was still a bit shaky from the war. Had a twitch he still couldn't stop, maybe from the phantom pains in his arm, and it got worse when he was hung over. Your mama knew what was what, but she was so glad we came home, said she'd take us however we came. As we walked up the center aisle of the church, the church we'd grown up visitin' and singin' in, I could see the welcome was conditional. People was whisperin' and pointin'. A child in the front had seen us first and pointed yellin', "Daddy, look at his face!" Nearly the whole congregation had turned 'round. Mil, he kept a walkin', head held high, pretendin' he didn't hear nothin'. He had you in his right arm, and his left sleeve'd been pulled up and tucked in by your mama. She said there was no need to hide your daddy's nub. It was what it was and she was proud of him. There were plenty of people whispering 'bout his arm, like we couldn't hear 'em in that old echoey church buildin'. Your mama guided us to a row in the middle, actin' like she didn't hear nothin', but I'm sure that weren't the case.

Well Pastor David had seen us enter, no doubt, and apparently he'd heard 'bout our escapades the night before. We'd been makin' quite a ruckus in town. He started right in on the evils of drinkin' and card playin'. Guess no one told him what trenches were like, or what it was like for your daddy layin' in a field hospital nearly bleedin' out or what it was like when they took what was left of his arm. One thing was certain, he didn't know that drinkin' and playin' cards were all we had to keep us sane. Weren't no books. There were girls, but your daddy never gave them a glance. Told me they didn't compare to what he had waitin'. In that way, he had your mama, too, along with drinkin' and card playin'.

Seemed like the whole sermon was on drinkin' and such. Kept yellin' all fire and brimstone like and lookin' our way. Now, I'd been called out in the Army for all sorts of stuff, some of which I did and others maybe I didn't, but I didn't expect to be called out in a sermon. No matter. I was there for your mama, but boy was I mad. After we stood up to leave, and folks came to see us said they was lookin' forward to seein' us at church and trustin' that we was gonna make our mama proud by straightenin' up our ways—somethin' 'bout last night bein' the last of those sorta things. I coulda taken that, but I couldn't take the lack of respect for your daddy. In one breath, they'd thank him for his service, as if you could thank someone for givin' up a arm, and in the next breath, they'd repeat warnins' 'bout us straightenin' up. Kirk was there. The choir Mil had grown up singin' in had been directed by him that day, as usual. He had his daughter with him and she weren't no little thing no more. She was all grown up. Boy did he keep his daughter from us. Guess she'd been starin'. That's what Rosie said after, anyways, and while Kirk needed to thank us for what we'd done for the country, we were in no way worthy of talkin' to his daughter. Well, I about had had it, and I guess Rosie recognized that. She came right up, interrupted Kirk, and asked us if we would come over to her place for lunch. Steered us right on outta there, with a smile on her face the whole time. That's how Rosie has always been. Don't matter what the situation, she's always got a smile. She buries a lot under that smile.

CHAPTER THIRTEEN

A Rose in the Darkness

Not many people lost more than Rosie. It's funny how those who suffer most are the most cheerful. I wasn't there when Rosie got the news, but I hear she got the news one day her brother was gone, and two days later she found out about Ricky. Buried 'em both in the same week. Well, weren't nothin' ta bury, but Ricky's mama and daddy needed a service and such, and it was nice to see their names in the town graveyard, even if we all knew there weren't nothin buried in those graves. Whatever was left of 'em was buried in a field in France.

Rosie told me once that it was your mama pulled her

through. Rosie had a place of her own then. Ricky's parents'd set her up there so Ricky would have a home to come back to and raise his family in. Your mama brought you and moved in with Rosie for some time after the news had come. Rosie said she has no memory of the days passin' after, but she remembers your mama comin' in with the baby and attachin' him so he could feed, since he was still a-nursin' baby, and then your mama would go on out to take care of you. She'd come back in later and get Rosie's baby to change him and care for him. Rosie said she wasn't able to do much in those days. Your mama would cook and bring food to Rosie and make her eat. She lost most of her world in one week—just her and the baby after that.

But Rosie was strong. Little by little, she started to get out of the darkness and come back to life. It was about this time that Goodwin decided to move hisself inta the big city. Well, his wife decided it was time. Didn't want their daughter marryin' none of us Levy boys, moved her to Gainesville where she thought her daughter could marry a better class of man. That meant Goodwin needed to sell his place, and Ricky's parents'd been thinkin' a lot 'bout how to set up Rosie to raise the baby on her own, seein' how she'd always been the independent type. They knew she'd want to support herself. So, they bought the bar and closed it down for a few weeks while Rosie and your mama fixed it up real nice. They repainted everything and gave it a sort of homey feel. They painted all the shudders green and named the place "Green Shudders." The tables were basic wood tables, similar to what a lotta folks had in their houses. They hung curtains they'd made themselves in the windows and rag rugs between all the tables that Ricky's mama'd woven by hand. Folks knew it was the same cook workin' the place, but with a lady overseein' things, folks got the idea it would be more nice-like. I hear tell that place was packed on openin' day, and it's been pretty much packed ever since. Rosie made all her customers feel welcomed, like they was visitin' at their friend's house. She'd shifted the menu to all home cookin'—corn bread, ham hocks, swamp cabbage, black-eyed peas, sweet potato pie, fried fish, and fried chicken. It became the place all the guys would go for lunch. They all called her "Sweetie," but they didn't mean nothin' by it. She was Ricky's girl, and they all knew it. They saw her as some sort of younger version of their mamas. She loved her guys, and always made 'em feel welcome and well fed. Didn't matter how much they ordered, they was always welcome to stay for as long as they liked. Didn't never rush no one out. Well, except for that one time Olmos had too much to drink, but he was back later that week, and he was welcome, too. Her place really was a second home to all the men in town, but like I said, Rosie was like a mama to 'em, and they needed that. I needed that.

At one point after we got back, someone'd opened up another place in town apparently. Guy'd passed through from some place up north and thought this little town needed a second place to eat on the main drag. Course, he figured no one would mind someone from outta town openin' up somethin' to rival Green Shudders, too. Man hadn't studied the town much, and it showed when he hired Lonny. That guy. Why he came back and Ricky didn't will always be a mystery. While prohibition hadn't hit yet, it still surprised me the amount of alcohol that man could get his hands on, and I was a drinkin' man myself. Well, he showed up to work the first few days. Cooked ham and all the fixins. He knew how to cook, I'll give him that. He'd be there all greasy with his big belly swayin' over the stove and he'd just be a singin'. His mama liked opera, I guess. Not sure why or how that happened. I hear it was a sight to see him there singin' in languages he didn't know, all opera like, and cookin' food for the locals who couldn't understand him neither. Weren't much of a crowd, but there was always a few people curious to try the new place in town.

Well, one day, Lonny'd shown up to work when maybe he shouldn't have. Boss'd been naggin' him for missin' work, so to work he went. When he got there all stinkin' drunk, guy chewed him out again and this time in front of customers. Lonny wasn't havin' it. Now the place was small, and customers could sit on their wooden stools at the counter and see right inta the kitchen. Word has it, he dropped his drawers right there in front'a the customers and took a shit in the pot of beans the boss'd been cookin'. Boss had his back to the kitchen, and bein' as folks weren't takin' kindly to him, they kept what they was seein' ta themselves, and bein' as the man was a idiot, he didn't see their raised eyebrows and take that as a sign of some sort and turn to see what they could see—big, ol' Lonny takin' a dump in the bean pot. Lonny finished up, stirred the beans, and served 'em up to folks, then he walked out the door and never looked back. Of course, no one was gonna eat those beans or anything else ever again from that man. That was the end of Rosie's competition. He didn't leave right away, of course. Tried to get somethin' goin' with Rosie, as if he had a chance. Kept comin' around at night when she was closin', wantin' to walk her home and talk business, he'd say. Course the town was dark and her house was empty, except for you, your mama and the little one. Weren't polite for a stranger to do. Like I said before, Rosie could take care of herself, but that time Ricky's daddy weren't havin' none of it. He'd seen what was goin' on, and he'd heard the things the man was sayin' 'bout Rosie when she weren't around, the plans the man had for her. Well one night, just before he would have closed and headed to Green Shudders, Ricky's daddy set hisself up on a stump out back of the place, where he knew the man would pass by, and sat there with the knife he used to castrate pigs, sharpinin' it on a stone. Just sat there starin' at the door, sayin' nothin' and sharpinin' the knife. Boy that man came out, took one look at Ricky's daddy and knew his time was up in the town. You don't mess with Rosie.

CHAPTER FOURTEEN

A Little Help from My Friends

After that first Sunday back at church with your mama and daddy, I knew Rosie saw me—really saw me. She knew I was hurtin', she knew I was a mess, and and it didn't bother her none. Told me once she woulda taken Ricky and Caleb home in any shape. Wouldn'ta cared if they was a mess inside or out, just to get the chance to hold 'em again.

Rosie took me in, so to speak. Weren't no one ever gonna stack up to Ricky. We never did when he was alive, and we certainly wasn't gonna after he'd died a hero's death. Some guys tried. Every now and then she'd give one a chance, but they rarely got past the first date before she'd kick 'em to the curb. No one could match Ricky. One guy didn't even make it to the first date. That guy missed the date. I was baby sittin' that night, so I saw Rosie waitin', lookin' all pretty, and the guy never came. Had the nerve to come by the next day and explain how he'd been arrested and jailed for the night but weren't his fault. Expected another chance at a date. I'd've chased him off, but Rosie didn't need my help. She always could take care of herself, and she knew her way 'round a shotgun right well. When Ricky's daddy or I stepped in, it was more to get in on the fun of chasin' the guy off. We needed Rosie, but she didn't need us. She could protect herself and the baby just fine. She'd been raised in the woods.

Folks often thought there was somethin' between me and Rosie in those days. Truth was, I knew I wasn't Ricky or Caleb. This was Ricky's girl, and she was the only childhood friend I had left except for your daddy. Rosie and I would stay up late just sittin' and talkin' 'bout the old days. We laughed 'bout that time she chased me and your daddy with mud pies. Chased us right inta a trap Ricky and Caleb had set up. Boy did we get muddy that day. We laughed 'bout the time she came in through the bathroom window when we was all sleepin' at Ricky's. He was the only one of us even had a bathroom inside. She remembered things that no one else knew. With her, I could relive my childhood, the childhood only the three of us remembered now, what with my mama and daddy gone. Bein' with Rosie was a relief from the memories and the nightmares, even though sometimes the memories included Ricky and Caleb, they was the good memories and it felt good to keep those memories goin', and to know Ricky's son would grow up hearin' 'bout his daddy and the fun we'd all had together.

I stayed a lot of nights at Rosie's back then. I'd work in the sawmill, eat at Green Shudders, then sleep out on Rosie's porch at night. I figured folks wouldn't talk if I was sleepin' on the porch, but they did and we didn't care. She was Ricky's and I knew it. Wouldn't never be nothin' between us.

CHAPTER FIFTEEN

Missing Piece

Your dad comin' home from the war was harder than he
ever let on. I'd been home for a while then, workin' at the
sawmill in town. After news'd reached the town 'bout Ricky
and Caleb, well, they was just glad to see one of us come back.
After we got your daddy settled at your mama's place in town,
I figured he'd want to get to work right away, but he didn't
think he could until he got some rest. Still was tremblin' and
shakin' mostly at night but some in the day too. He needed
some time with your mama, and she'd saved some money, what
with me havin' helped with bills for a while. Seemed right after

all he'd been through if he took a week or two 'fore he went lookin' for somethin'. I knew they was lookin' for another guy at the mill and promised your dad I'd get him hired. Didn't turn out that way. Sure, your daddy'd lost half of his left arm, but well, it was his left arm and he was right-handed. We knew that weren't nothin' a Levy boy couldn't handle. Could overcome anything with the right mind set. My daddy always said, "God made dogs with three legs and a extra." That was his way of sayin' that a dog could live with three legs. Said it after we'd seen a dog runnin' 'round on three legs, I guess. I figured your daddy was better'n a dog and he'd figure it out. 'Sides, he was just like me—he was my twin. Everyone knew we was hard workers, and missin' part of a arm or a messed up nose weren't goin' to slow down how much work we could do. I didn't care none what your daddy looked like. I knew he was a workin' man.

Turns out they did care. Boss man took one look at Mil's arm and face and wasn't havin' any of it. Your daddy asked if he could show them. Offered to work for free for a day just to show 'em, but well, they wasn't havin' it. Was pretty discouragin' for your daddy. When he walked away, well, I just couldn't take it. I walked right out with him and never looked back. Couldn't see fit to work in a place that wouldn't even give my brother a chance. Rejectin' him is rejectin' me, I said. Well, with a bit more color to it.

No matter, your daddy was busy gettin' to know your mama again and had managed a bit of work from Ricky's daddy, so he was gettin' by for a few weeks at least. Ricky's daddy probably didn't need a guy workin' for 'em, but he liked havin' Mil around. I couldn't find work, especially when word got around town that I wouldn't work without your daddy. Word always spread like wildfire in our small town. With no work to tie me down, I started hitchin' my way down past Rosewood. Down there, I had the closest thing to a beach, or my version of a beach; we called it Shellmound. What I've heard tell is that Indians use to live on that there body of water, where the river meets the sea, and they would pile up their trash—broken pottery, arrowheads, empty shells and such. These Indians were there such a long time ago that no one remembers them and the garbage pile they left was as big as a hill, only we don't have no hills in that area. Trees have grow'd on the hill of trash now, and bushes and such. Wildlife has moved in and claimed the hill as a home. Nature has a way of overcomin', and she sure did here. I like to call them the trash Indians, but I suppose they had a proper name, just not one we learned in school. Like I said, they'd been forgotten to time and only left trash behind.

Well, on top of this man-made hill is the best view in the county, and not many know about it even now, but back then I had it almost to myself. I would go to the top of this old heap of trash and sit on the edge and look out over the estuary watchin' the birds fishin'. I could see the brown water of the Suwannee mixin' in with the water of the Atlantic in between my hill and the smaller barrier islands off of the coast. Little palm trees and underbrush grew on some of the islands, creatin' a nice view, but some of them was just white beach covered in little birds in the right season. We never did canoe there much. Tide was such a bitch there. If you didn't watch yourself, you could get out on a island and the water would almost all leave, leavin' behind a thick, canoe suckin' mud that no man wants to battle. So mostly I just sat and looked and thought. Thought about the war, 'bout my friends I left behind and 'bout your dad. Prohibition hadn't started quite yet, but it was a-cookin', so I tended to do my drinkin' there too, where I could do it without judgment or a audience. Just me and my thoughts. The sun shinin' off those muddy waters and the breeze comin' off those little islands had a way of makin' all things right in the world, even when I knew nothin' was right.

It was in this spot that I first met Josh, or Uncle Josh as you always used to call him. When I got to my spot, he was there leaning against a tall cedar tree to get outta the breeze. I sat down and ignored him and opened up my bottle, more than a little annoyed my spot had been found by another guy. When I looked up later, there was a huge bird just a sittin' a few branches above me. His pencil like legs stood on the branch as it swayed in the wind, and his toes held on while he slept with his beak tucked inta his wing, his neck all turned unnatural like to get it there. That was when Josh came over, laughed at the sleepin' bird and asked if I minded if he joined me. Of course, I did mind, but mama raised me to be polite, so I said he was welcome to have a seat. He looked grubby in his ratty jeans and white, long sleeve shirt that showed the effects of hard work. To tell you the truth, I didn't expect much from him. He was only the guy who was taken' my spot from me.

And then he got out a sack of corncake and ham. I hadn't eaten in a day or two. He must've known I was hungry or I was starin'. Hard to say. I hadn't seen ham in a bit. Well, he didn't say a word, just handed me half of his ham and some corn cake. We ate in silence, both of us men who knew the value of food, and I shared my liquor with him.

When the food was gone, and both of us had sat in silence for a bit, he asked me where I'd served. He knew just from lookin' at me that I had. I told him I was with the 332nd in Italy. He was with the 369th under Pershing—it was the first Negro regiment and boy was he proud of that. I asked him how things was goin' for him now that he was back and he said things weren't too bad. He had work in Rosewood. The town was up and comin'. Some folks needed his help fishin' and such in Cedar Key. When I told him I was between work, left out the part about quitting the one job cuz they wouldn't hire your daddy, he said he'd let me know if he heard of a spot for me. Of course, I let him know I couldn't take a job without your daddy and that lots of folks wouldn't hire him given his injuries, but that he was willin' to work a day for free to prove hisself. He said, "If the white folks in CK would hire me, they'd probably hire your brother" and we laughed it off.

"Let's go fishin'," he said, and he led me 'bout a mile from the hilltop through some sandy trails lined with pine straw and palm leaves. We came up on this old dock that was mostly rotten and made ourselves some cane poles with some string and hooks he'd brought in his sack. Became a joke for me later—Josh has everything we need in that there sack. No worries. Well, after the poles was made weren't no problem to find bait. Lots of little crabs had taken cover from the cold inta the warmth of the mud. They made for easy bait. The water in this spot was also brown, but the cross breeze made the water shimmer and blue herons was tip toein' 'round the edges of the pond lookin' for their dinner in the tall grass around the edge. We sat on what was left of the dock and fished, neither of us talkin'. We both caught red fish and made quick work of cleanin' 'em when we was ready. I started up a fire back near the trail. Found a nice cleared off area with a view of the pond. Always felt good lookin' out at the water, and I wanted to look at the water while my fish was cookin'. We cooked the fish on a flat stone down in the coals of the fire, and Josh pulled some cold swamp cabbage outta his sack while I finished cookin' the fish. We dined like kings that night. Swamp kings, maybe, but it sure felt good to have two meals in one day like that.

As night fell, we talked about the war and the ones who didn't come back with us. I told him about Ricky and Caleb, and he told me about his friends who hadn't come back. He blamed Pershing for that. Said he didn't care how many of his black men he lost. Maybe, but I said most of them generals didn't care how many of us they lost, long as they got their objective done. They'd just keep throwin' guys up mountains and at barbed wire until eventually some of 'em climbed over enough bodies to break through.

When the alcohol was gone, and the story tellin' was finished, we slept under the stars on beds of pine straw. Stayed out there all weekend, fishin' and cookin' over a fire, 'til Josh had to head off to work on Monday mornin'. He took work more seriously than I did, and I took drinkin' more seriously than he did. When he left, he told me to come back Friday, and to bring your daddy. Thought he'd be able to find us some work, said he'd ask 'round for us.

That's where things turned 'round for us again. Josh found us some work fishin'. He'd put in a good word for us and when they heard of your daddy's willingness to work for free for a day—that got us a spot. Your daddy was true to his word. He could haul in more nets with his one and a half arms than the other guys could with their two arms. He was determined to provide for his girls, that and I think he needed to prove it to hisself. He needed to see he could keep up with the rest of the guys, and that drive made him a better workman, better husband, and better daddy than any of the other guys in Cedar Key. Once your daddy worked for a week or two, commuting back and forth to your mama's place in Chiefland, he found a little place for all of us on the island. Those are the days and the daddy I want you to remember, so let me tell you a little more about it.

CHAPTER SIXTEEN

In Between Times

It's funny what you remember. One of my biggest memories of this time was your mama in her big, floppy, pink hat. Boy did she love that hat. We was all there when she bought it. Tried it on in one of those shops in the wooden buildings that lined the streets of Cedar Key, right on the water. Put it on her pretty head and asked your daddy if she could buy it. Josh and I chimed in with "It's not could ya buy it but should ya." Josh and me just laughed and laughed. Funniest lookin' hat. Course, after that, your daddy had to get it for her, and she wore it daily. Claimed it kept the sun outta her eyes. Sure did love to stick it to me and Josh, your mama did.

Times were good then. We could buy hats and other silly things. Your daddy and mama rented that little house right on the water on First Street, maybe you remember it. It was one set up on concrete blocks, with a little porch in the front and a closed porch on the side, all painted red. It was the nicest house we'd ever had to ourselves; course, all three of us guys was chippin' in for the rent then. It was the only place I'd ever lived that weren't whitewashed—sure was proud of it. Wished mama and daddy had lived to see us livin' so well. We could sit out on the closed porch and watch the dolphins jumpin' in the waves almost daily. Those dolphins would come right up inta the shallows and herd fish in to eat 'em, sorta like a fishin' expedition for dolphins. Never ceased to amaze you.

When me and Josh was workin' and livin' in Cedar Key, we stayed in the porch so as you could have a room and your mama and daddy could have the other. When we was workin' then, we would walk inta town. We didn't always fish. Only in season, mostly red fish and mullet, or whatever we wanted when the game wardens weren't lookin'. Some things never change. There was 'bout a hundred of us guys fishin' in the area then. We'd all head out in the mornin' and use these big nets, damn near caught everything movin' in the ocean. Sometimes, we caught dolphins, but we tried not to. We'd be out there all day usin' nets in our spots, and haulin' in our catch end of day. Felt like I was part of a big group'a guys again. Felt good. We was all workin' for the same thing—catch as many fish as we could so as to put food on the table and beer in our stomachs. The town was full of us guys, and some guy who was a dentist, but didn't practice bein' a dentist no more, 'cept for friends and family. We weren't friends and family sorta guys, but no matter. My mama always said our teeth was so strong, just like we was, and we didn't need no doctor or no dentist. Seems she was right, seein' as the doc couldn't save her from the flu, and my teeth is all still here.

Anyways, we stayed in our fishin' circle of guys and didn't mind those livin' up on the hill none. They liked our fish and we liked their island, so we was just fine. The railroad came to the island back then, and there was seven fish houses up by the tracks for all of us guys to load the fish on the trains. At the end of the day, you'd see us all lined up, just a bringin' our fish in to be weighed and shipped. Trains took the fish all the way to New York City, and some other places. It weren't pretty work, but it was work and we always had food. We was proud of ourselves then, workin' hard and makin' ends meet, just like our daddy taught us.

Aside from fishin', we pretty much did any kind of work we could get our hands on, or hand in your daddy's case. We worked buildin' houses, when there was houses to be built. Sometimes, we was workin' for the Standard Oil Dock Station and Marina downtown. All those guys out fishin' mostly had gasoline engines on their boats by then, so they was needin' gas, storage for boats, and boat repairs, and all of that was stuff me, your daddy, and Josh was good at. Well, while we'd had experience with all kinds of work durin' the war, your daddy was the one that had worked on engines some, and boy could he keep an engine tickin'. Kept him workin' even when it was stormin' so there was no fishin'.

When we wasn't fishin' or fixin' things, a lot of the time we worked for this company that made fibers and ropes outta palm trees. Craziest thing. I'd grown up in the woods and had no idea those things was useful. Turns out they was so useful that those fibers kept the Standard Manufacturing Company afloat during and after the war, and even through the depression. We cut the trees for 'em, or whatever else they needed. Got those fibers outta the tree, and the fiber would go all 'round the world, even as far as Australia. They made all sorts'a things outta those fibers, like brushes and stuff. Who knew you could make so much outta a tree that grows like a weed. It was good work, and it was honest work. After the problems your daddy had when he first got back, we was just grateful to have so much work to do.

Wherever we was workin', life was pretty good in Cedar Key, lookin' back. In the winter, we ate oysters and fish, and in the summer, we'd go scallopin', though we had to head north a ways to scallop. That was the finest of the fishin' jobs. We'd have to go out on the boss' boat and strip down to our skivies and we'd dive down and get scallops. We got really good at holdin' our breath. Your daddy always said it was the only job he ever got paid to work in his skivies.

With their bein' so much food in the ocean, we ate pretty well most nights, especially when your mama was cookin'. We'd fish, harvest oysters, and put traps out for crabs right off the back yard, well, we went a bit further for oysters. We'd just canoe a bit out for the crab traps or paddle out to our favorite oyster harvestin' spots when tide was low so we could walk and get ourselves some. "Only in months that have 'r's," your mama used to say. We stuck with her rules, for the most part. We was a family, after all. When we didn't work, we played all day. Ricky's family still had canoes down there and we got to use them whenever we wanted to. Your daddy mostly liked to stay with you and your mama at that point. Me and Josh would go out fishin' for the family and playin' on the off-shore islands, like we always had growin' up.

Sometimes people would get all worked up over Josh and me bein' friends. By that time, we was inseparable. Neither of us had a woman, and didn't figure that was changin', so we stayed with the family we did have. Way I figured it, we both served and we both grew up in Levy, we was the same guy. Just in different skin. Not everyone saw it that way. If it weren't such a small town, might've been a problem, but everyone knew me and Mil. They'd seen the burns on your daddy's face and figured he deserved all the help he could get, even if the guy fishin' and huntin' with his brother was black, must be helpin' provide food for Mil and his family. They didn't get me and Josh hangin' 'round each other all the time, guess their minds was too small to picture black guys and white guys bein' equal friends. They'd also heard stories from my time in the war, probably most of 'em was just rumor, but those rumors made 'em figure they should let me be, I guess. Figured I wasn't right in the head, and I suppose I wasn't.

One time we was out on our favorite barrier island, the one

we went to when your daddy proposed to your mama, only we was fishin' separately on different sides of the island. This time I'd seen a bunch of conchs. Musta' been matin' season, assumin' they have a matin' season. I ditched my fishin' plans and just started grabbin' all the conchs I could. Figured your mama could make up some of that conch soup she made so well. Maybe she'd even make some of her famous biscuits to thank me for gettin' all these conchs. When the bag I had with me was full, I walked the long way 'round the island, watchin' a school of dolphins jumpin' offshore. You never tire of that sight.

When I made my way 'round the short end of the pencil-shaped island, there was a group of men just a beatin' on Josh and callin' him awful names. I'd seen them, but they hadn't seen me, so I set my conch bag in the shade of a tree and stepped inta the brush and trees that run down the center of the island. Planned on usin' my sharpshooter skills. There were very few rocks on the island, big ones that is. The shore is lined with little stones and broken shells that will pierce your foot if you're not careful, but not good throwin' rocks, and as I didn't have a gun with me, throwin' something just right seemed to be my best option. While there weren't any big rocks, there was a pile of bricks that had washed over from Atsena Otie when the houses and factories'd been damaged in the hurricane of '96 and other storms. I got me four of those bricks—one for each guy—and snuck up on them through the brush. Figured I needed to even the playin' field. I aimed just right, and I got the biggest of the guys square on the back of the head with the brick, and just as soon as they could turn 'round, I got a second guy on the forehead. I came out in a rush on the last two, and the third guy got me right on the nose, but I managed to bang him on the back of the head with a brick still, and by then Josh was up takin' on the last guy. The biggest guy was still on his face in the sand, and these last guys figured they weren't evenly matched, even with their only bein' two of us, and they took off sprintin' and shoutin' some racist slurs on their way out to their boat. Josh and me, we tied up those last two guys. When we got back to shore, I mentioned them bein' out there to the local police, said they might wanna send someone to get 'em. They'd been causin' trouble out there. After that, Josh and me stuck together in Cedar Key. Them guys weren't from our area. Visitors from outta state, but we weren't takin' no chances. That night I heard stories all stretched to say I'd taken on six or more guys all by myself and left 'em tied up out there to die in the sun, stripped down to their skivvies. Josh was the only witness, and he thought it was funny to hear the stories grow, so he let it be and folks figured I was bein' modest, if I denied the stories. Kinda helped my reputation in town and kept people at a distance, which was always nice, especially when those folks liked to walk the town at night in white sheets with torches in their hands.

Anyways, we wasn't raised to hate people for their skin color. Mostly mama and daddy said to be nice to people that was nice to us. When I was in Italy, there was this fellow, Brown. We all laughed at him being brown and being named

Brown. Guess it weren't so funny to him, but he took it well. He was 'bout the nicest guy in the unit. Figured he was outnumbered, I guess, but he said his mama raised him right and that's why he was so nice. He was the guy could always get something for us to drink, knew where the girls was at, and always had extra paper to write home. He was from up north somewhere, and his family had some money. Any money was more than I had growin' up. Guess that's how he ended up with the Red Cross attached to a unit of white guys, cuz most guys was in the segregated units, even in the Red Cross. Anyways, I never forgot his kindness and friendship, so I guess I didn't think nothin' 'bout Josh bein' a different color than me. That's why 1923 was such a surprise to me, but I shoulda seen it comin'.

Not so many of those things happened to me and Josh in Cedar Key after that. Word got 'round. Me and Josh was family with you, your mama and daddy. We looked out for each other, and we provided for each other in the fish we caught and the money we earned. We watched you take your runnin' first steps along the grassy field by the salt water. At night, we would hit the bars together, well at least two of us hit the bars. Your daddy was tryin' ta keep a handle on his drinkin' for you and your mama's sake, so mostly he drank at home when he wrote so as the writin' kept his drinkin' under control, cuz if he drank too much, he couldn't write no more.

He used to write about you. Bet you didn't know that. At night sometimes, after you was in bed, we'd sit on the front porch and talk. On one of those nights, hell, probably on a few of 'em, he told us 'bout these books he was writin' 'bout a girl. This girl could save the world, he'd say. She was young and smart, pretty, too. This girl was so smart, she went to school all the way in Atlanta. She got herself so smart from readin' all these books, she even learned the secret of flyin'. This girl, she'd fly into the houses of the rich folks up in Atlanta and sneak out the food and clothes they weren't usin' and she'd bring 'em ta the poor kids in the normal neighborhoods. Josh and I told him weren't no one gonna believe folks were sittin' 'round with extra food and clothes, but Mil said it was true. Guess Brown had lived in one of those houses somewhere up North. Mil had seen guys like that in the war, too, been pulled outta Yale and Harvard to go fight in the war. None of us had grown up knowin' that kinda comfort, but we was doin' okay. After all, we had a house right on the water and all the fish and seafood we could eat. Seein' as Josh and I had our other place we built out on Shell Mound, you could even say we had two houses. But anyway, we liked the idea of you stealin' from the rich and givin' to the poor. We could see you as a savior of sorts, or a modern-day girl Robin Hood.

Anyways, weren't all good in that time. Least not for your mama. She and your daddy lost a few babies at Cedar Key. They wanted more kids so badly, but her body just couldn't keep 'em. Most folks didn't know she'd even been in a family way, but we knew as we was livin' under one roof most of the time, see'n how work was easier to get to from the Cedar Key house than it was walkin' from Shell Mound, but each time she'd go through another loss, we'd go back to Shell Mound for a week or two. Your daddy didn't ask us to, we just figured they needed some time alone, seein' how upset your mama was. Sometimes we'd take you with us. You could walk pretty far in those days, 'specially if it meant gettin' time alone with your favorite uncles. Josh and me would sleep out on the porch those nights, get all ate up by mosquitos, but we didn't care none. It was just nice havin' you 'round, and we didn't have more 'n one, small room. Wanted you to be like a little princess, gettin' her own room when she visited.

You liked bein' out in the woods then, seein' how your folks had a place in town. Josh and I had built our place ourselves. Course, we was buildin' houses sometimes for work, so we sorta knew what we was doin'. We didn't have much to work with, though, so we aimed for something like what I'd read Thoreau had in his time at Walden. Like I said, it had one room, but inside we'd fit two cots, a small stove for heat and cookin', and two chairs. We'd move them out on the porch, like Thoreau did, when we wanted to sit and look at the water or watch the birds. When we was livin' out there without you, we'd get up before the sun and walk into Cedar Key for work. On the weekends, we'd just sit and fish in the pond. The pond was fed by a tidal creek, so it was well stocked. There were hogs, too, so sometimes we'd go get one in the woods, and we'd take some of them to cook over the fire at night, the rest we'd salt down and store in the barn we'd built. Your daddy would make fun of us 'bout that barn. Turned out a little bigger than the house, and seein' as we didn't have no animals for the barn, your daddy always said we'd be better off bein' our own animals and livin' in the barn. I didn't care none. The barn was a good place to store our gear and to keep the salted pork and such. Your daddy didn't laugh when he'd come and get some of that pork in exchange for some of your mama's cookin'. That's how it was. We traded, we helped each other and we gave to each other. It was good times and we was a family then. That's what you need to remember, even if you was just a little one.

CHAPTER SEVENTEEN

Canoe Trips

This was a point in your life when spendin' time with your two favorite uncles was all you wanted to do when you wasn't in school. One time, when you was still a little thing, we went campin' for the night, just you and me. Josh was visitin' his family that weekend, and your mama and daddy were needin' some time alone. You and I picked up Ricky's canoe and took off for our own weekend on our private island. Course, it wasn't really ours, we just said that cuz we was the only ones there every time we went. The water was a cloudy, blue and brown, and I can still smell the salt water. Had a different smell bein' as it was a estuary and not the ocean. You laughed at all the mullet jumpin' outta the water, but you loved seein' the spoonbill rosettes. Your mama taught you the names of all the shore birds, and you loved teachin' me. That name stayed with me all these years cuz of how you laughed at the spoon-shaped bills of the birds. I don't remember the rest you taught me. There was oyster somethin' birds on our island. Don't right remember what their name was, just that you told me they nested on shore and ate oysters. They weren't as funny, so I just recall you tellin' me and not what you said. Looked so cute when you said it. You loved teachin' me when you was little.

You and me digged up some oysters off-shore and caught fish together in my net. Your mama sent us with some biscuits and cumquats. She always sent the best food when you went with me, but that weren't why I took you with me. You was my favorite girl. I always used to tell you that, not sure you remember, but I did mean it. Still do. No girl ever held my heart in her hands like you did and still do. We sat out by the campfire together that night, lookin' at the stars and makin' names for ones we didn't know the names of. The water was like a black mirror, reflectin' the moon and stars and any lights comin' from the city bars. We'd watch that mirror and you'd wonder about what was swimmin' under the surface. Sometimes we'd even fish for sharks together at night, you stayed safely on the shore (mama's orders), but you loved to watch me pull in a shark for a late dinner.

We wasn't fishin' ta bring food home that weekend, we was

just bein' us on our island. You pretended you was a pirate held up with his store of rum. Made me laugh. At night over the fire while we was cookin' that shark we caught, you asked me to tell you all about the night your daddy proposed to your mama. You laughed so much 'bout that turtle. You insisted I show you where your daddy had buried that smelly, old turtle. Weren't nothin' left of the grave marker your mama made, but you still liked the story.

That mornin' you woke me up just a yellin' there was a rattlesnake in the tree. You hated snakes. Got that from your daddy. He always said, "the only good snake is a dead snake." Course, he wasn't afraid of them, he just killed every one he came across. Your mama got to where she was pretty good at cookin' up rattlesnake meat. Your daddy's insistence on killin' 'em turned inta fear in you. Well, that mornin', you was all worked up about a snake in the trees. I got a long stick and my knife. I crept up to that tree, still wiping the sleep outta my eyes. I was ready for a fight and thinkin' of snake for lunch, but when I got closer, I just fell down laughin' at you. Made you so mad. Turned out what you saw as a snake was the sun shinin' just right through the palm frowns on to the branch that lay behind the palm frowns, made a striped effect on the branch, looked somethin' like a snake—well, at least it did to you that day. I promised not to tell your daddy. One person laughin' was enough for you that weekend. Even with me makin' light of your mistake, you still didn't want to go back that weekend, but I wanted you to be at school Monday mornin', and I knew your mama would want you home with enough time to clean you up and have you lookin' like a lady at school, not that you had any of those kids fooled. They knew who you ran with.

Other weekends we went out to Atsena Otie. Used to be a lot on that island even in my parents' day. In fact, when I was a little guy, there was still 'bout thirty families on that island. Some of 'em even had two story houses, like you can still see over on Second Street in Cedar Key. Had chickens out in their yards and grew all kinds of fruit. Even guavas. Never heard tell 'bout guavas until Ricky told us 'bout 'em. His mom'd brought 'em back from some trip she went on, and then she heard they grew 'em out on Atsena. That was one of the few times we boys went out to Atsena. We rowed ourselves out there one night and raided some guava to try. Didn't take more'n one each, boy did they taste good on the way back. Anyways, that's why your daddy and Ricky never wanted to take the girls out to Atsena. Too many people a-nosen' 'round.

Well, by the time you was the lady I was takin' out canoein', there weren't much left on the island. Really, there weren't that much left when we was boys, either. That hurricane in 1896 had left an effect and many of the businesses had been moved across the water to the main island. Wished I'd been there to see that. Anyways, you and me, we'd go out there to Atsena "artifact huntin'," which is what you called it. You'd find bricks from the pencil factory or tools from the other factories, even a bible from a church once, all of which had either washed away or been moved across to Cedar Key. Those were the sorts of things that got your attention back then. One time we went out there and we was gettin' conchs on the backside of the island when you spotted a hand comin' up outta the mud along the shore not far from us. A storm had gone through not long before and that day we was walkin' in the mud pretty far out from Otie's shore. Well, musta been a Indian graveyard and the storm had uncovered it. I thought you'd be scared, but you wasn't. You was fascinated by the skeleton hand you saw. Had to get a closer look. Turned out there was twelve skeletons all lined up, parts of 'em just pokin' up through the mud. Seein' as how we'd already found and explored the official graveyard left on the island, and now there was skeletons pokin' up through the mud along the shore, you decided the island was haunted. That became one of your favorite places to go. We'd go through the graveyard and find the little graves of the babies. I think that helped you with all of the babies your mama lost. Sort of saw it as a normal part of life. There was one grave you liked in particular. Was bigger'n the rest. Had a poem written on it. Went somethin' like:

> Tears fell, when thou wert dying,
> From eyes unused to weep,
> And long when thou art lying,
> Will sadness o'er us creep.

Made you feel sorta sad-like. Used to tell me stories you made up of the man musta written it. You figured he lost his wife, as many did, when she was young and givin' birth, like many on Otie had. Sometimes you'd even make up names for the baby, lettin' the baby live to be raised by his daddy. Other times the baby died too, leavin' the daddy in the kinda sorrow many men lived in at that time. You was always creative as a child.

Back then we'd come back from our canoe trips, whether they was overnight or just day trips, and you'd sit on the back porch and ask your daddy to tell you ghost stories while you stared out across the water to Atsena Otie. Your mama didn't think that was right. She wanted you to be some kind of lady, and she was afraid you'd get nightmares, but you didn't. I told her you was stuck with too many men in your life to end up a lady. Besides, ladies didn't have no fun at all, and we was havin' a great time out canoein', fishin', and listenen' to your daddy's stories.

CHAPTER EIGHTEEN

Rosewood and Recovery

Like I said before, Me and Mil, we never gave a hoot if a fella was black or white. Sometimes our daddy had worked with black fellas when he was turpentinin'. Mama told us that God made some people black and it didn't matter. We weren't around a lot of black guys back then when we was little guys, since the towns was mostly segregated, so was the schools, but we figured mama knew what she was talkin' 'bout. Ricky told us that underneath a black fella was the same as a white fella, and, well, Ricky always knew what he was talkin' 'bout too so, given the way we was raised, we accepted there were people who looked different than us but they was the same. Besides, when I got back, Josh was the only person, 'side from your daddy, who understood what I was dealin' with. He knew where your daddy had been. We didn't talk about the details, we just knew. Josh couldn't sleep well, and I knew why. I knew the ghosts that kept him up because I had ghosts of my own.

Well, while Josh and me had us that little place out near Shell Mound, he would still go home to his family in Rosewood when he got the chance. Wasn't a long walk, and his mom and dad still lived out there. He had plenty of aunts, uncles, cousins, and siblings, and some of them had kids, too. Josh never did have good timin'. He was fortunate enough to come home from the war. His bad timing held out at home; when he went back to visit his mama one week and get some of her good cookin', a woman in the neighborin' white town of Sumner accused a black man from Rosewood of comin' inta her house and rapin' her. Rosewood was a pretty tight community, and they all knew the dangers of goin' inta Sumner for anything other than business. Folks in Sumner weren't real open sorta people. It seems like a man from Rosewood wouldn't go take what he wants from anyone or anything in Sumner. Most folks in Cedar Key, when they was bein' honest, said this white woman was probably foolin' 'round with a white man and got caught. Had to tell her husband somethin'. Husband believed her. Pretty soon all of Sumner was in a uproar. It didn't take much back then to turn a group of angry, white men against a town of black folks.

That angry, white mob brought itself on over to Rosewood demanding justice and when the town wouldn't give up a man as the guilty party, since there was no such man, the mob turned on the whole town. They burned down houses, stores, churches—even if people was inside of the buildings. No matter. They burned the buildings just the same.

Folks started pouring out inta the scrubs surrounding Rosewood. Figured if they could make it to Gainesville, they'd be okay. Josh told me he managed to get his sister and her two kids out, but the rest he couldn't save or they went in another direction in the swamp. Man lost his whole family in a matter of minutes. His brother had been one of the first to go down. That guy had fought off the Huns in France, but he was unarmed and couldn't take down a group of armed men on his own. He was lynched in a tree before Josh'd even seen him. Well, Josh was runnin' with both of his nieces through the woods with his sister. Somehow his sister got separated a bit. The white men found her and when Josh came up, one niece in each hand, that mob was standin' 'round watchin' a white fella rape his sister. Josh told the girls to be quiet and hide in the palmettos. He figured he could take those men out one at a time if he could take them by surprise. Well those girls saw what was happenin' to their mama and started wailin' while Josh was on the other side of the group, comin' up behind 'em. Those men grabbed the girls, no bigger than six or seven, and started pinin' 'em down for the same treatment as their mama. Josh knew he couldn't wait. He came outta those bushes and started takin' out the men between him and the girls, but he wasn't armed and they were. The girls and their mama were killed instantly by the men on top of 'em, although the insult to their bodies didn't stop. In his grief and anger, with no weapons, two of the men were able for a moment to hold Josh down besides his sister's body. They was takin' off his pants, gettin' ready to mutilate his body and hang him from a tree, as they had done to many others already that day. When he realized he couldn't save any of the girls, something clicked in his head and he fought his way out from those guys and ran like hell through the scrubs and swamp to get to our shack. He figured together we could find a way out.

We didn't think our place would be safe for either of us, and we weren't sure where in the woods the men were towards Sumner, Rosewood, or on to Gainesville, so we tracked in the other direction towards your daddy and Cedar Key. As soon as he saw Josh all bloody and half naked, he knew what needed to be done. We put Josh in a large trunk your mama had in the living room under some quilts your mama and her mama had made, and we carried him out to the car that belonged to our employer. We wasn't supposed to use it on our own, but we decided to take our chances. We took off with some bottles of rum in hand. When we were stopped on 24, the only highway leavin' Cedar Key, we acted drunk, which wasn't hard for us, and told the men searchin' cars we was headin' ta Gainesville to find us some ladies. Wanted to keep the New Year's celebratin' goin', seein' as it was still early January. We cheered the men on and told them they should check down by the schoolhouse. We knew they wouldn't find nobody there and thought a little misguidance would give everyone runnin' for their lives a bit more time to get to safety.

We drove the rest of the way with our headlights out, hopin' ta go unnoticed as we made our way to Archer. Word hadn't spread to Archer yet about what was goin' on, so we were able to drive from there on inta Gainesville with no worries. Well, we was worried, but weren't no problems. Josh got out of the trunk in the back seat of the car once we left Levy County and directed us to his second aunt's house on the south side of Gainesville.

There was no comin' back to Levy county after that for Josh. A man can't live where it ain't safe to raise a family, and ain't no man livin' where he watched family members killed. He was the only one to make it to Gainesville outta his whole family. A handful of others from Rosewood made it. They compared stories and knew there was no one to go back for, and no chance they could go back and bury the dead without joinin' the dead in the woods and the swamps. Even the sheriff was in on the killin' spree, and some of the local government, so there was no hope for help in givin' the dead a proper burial, or in gettin' the houses and land back. All was lost to the hate and the anger of a white mob led by a cheatin' woman.

Josh didn't talk about Rosewood much after that, so maybe this is your first time hearin' 'bout it. Man couldn't deal with losin' everything and everybody, so he kinda boxed it up and only brought it out when we was alone, sittin' 'round the fire here and there. Told me when we was in DC that he read a poem by some guy named Claude. Hit home for him, seein' as he'd fought for his country and then still lost his family in a fight he couldn't win, and he couldn't even get revenge. What happened to your mama when she was a little girl was horrible, but we took that piece of shit out. These men was livin' life and enjoyin' themselves. They would live out their lives with no recompense. Well, the poem went somethin' like this, and it expressed how Josh felt more than he coulda said himself:

> If we must die, let it not be like hogs
> Hunted and penned in an inglorious spot . . .
> Like men we'll face the murderous, cowardly pack,
> Pressed to the wall, dying, but fighting back!

His brother died like a hog off in the scrubs of Florida and never even got himself a proper burial. Man served his nation. Shoulda had a chance to fight back, and even years after Josh didn't have a chance to fight back, just focused on the fight to keep food on his table.

We didn't last long in Cedar Key after that. Turns out some of your daddy's neighbors had seen us sneakin' Josh inta the house and the trunk outta the house, and they knew what had happened. Word spread fast. Pretty soon folks dressed in white sheets were burnin' crosses in your daddy's front yard and paintin' things like "N- - - -r lovr" on the side of the house. They spelled like that, too. Couldn't even spell lover right. Your mama couldn't take the stress and the hate around her. She always said that was what caused her to miscarry that one time, but lots of folks lost babies back then, and she'd already lost a few, so I don't know.

Your daddy couldn't keep your mama and you in a neighborhood where you wasn't safe, so one night we packed everything we could up inta a car borrowed from Ricky's family, and we all left under the cover of darkness. Figured no one would see us if we left quietly and went to a place we knew was empty to rest up for the night. We headed to old man Caruso's land. He'd lost his boys, one to the flu and one to the war, so we thought he might need field hands.

CHAPTER NINETEEN

Makin' Money

I'd lost my best friend. He was still around, but at that time travelin' to Gainesville was a rare occasion. Might could make it there a few times a year. Couldn't relax at home, neither, seein' as I couldn't look at my neighbors the same. There was no way of knowin' who had been involved, or who wished that they had been involved, without puttin' myself and all of you inta danger. So, for a long time we just kept to ourselves on Caruso's land. We worked, we farmed, and we started makin' our own moonshine. There was good money in moonshine 'bout that time, but I'm gettin' ahead of myself again.

Work for old man Caruso wasn't gonna make us wealthy by no means, but we was safe and had some food, so we took it. Weren't any other options. Man let us set up camp on his land, livin' in a shack some of his field hands had built years before.

Josh was my buddy. He understood us stayin' in Levy without sayin'. 'Sides, we had no real connections in Gainesville and a man's got to be sure his kin is fed. Josh had family to get him a job on the south side of town, but there weren't no work there for your daddy, seein' as he was white and he was missing half an arm. Anyways, we was still friends. Grief changes a man, makes it harder to be open to new friends. I'm tellin' you this because you've had your share of grief, and I don't want you to end up a lonely, old, son of a bitch like me. Keep the friends you have, even if life moves them on.

Well, Josh wasn't comin' back from Gainesville, and after a while, we realized we weren't gettin' enough work from Caruso to really set ourselves up and keep you full, so me, your daddy, your mama and you was left to think on where to find work, and we did a lot of thinkin'. Weren't no one else hirin', especially not with your daddy's arm and his face lookin' the way it did, and I wasn't workin' for no man wouldn't hire Mil. He was blood and I was stickin' with him.

That's when I remembered Goodwin's "fortress of booze." That shed had stood the test of time. Got me wonderin' if Goodwin'd ever gotten a start on a real still. I asked Rosie if I could take a look in there. The place was full of spiders, which had kept her out. Girl wasn't afraid of nothin' 'cept

121

hairy spiders. Guess I can't blame her none.

Sure enough, there was a pair of six-barrel, copper pots just a sittin' there given house to spiders. Back then, guys used tin pots and radiator coils cuz they was cheaper, but it made for bad shine, could make a man sick. Weren't like Goodwin to go cheap on nothin' and he sure didn't on his still. Course, I knew we couldn't set up shop there behind Rosie. If the Feds came through, they'd take her place from her, send her to jail 'n put the baby in a home if'n we got caught. Wouldn't even let me be seen gettin' the still from what turned out to really be the fortress of booze. Went to Ricky's daddy. Man solved all of our problems. We was carless. Your daddy had sold most of what we had to put food in you and your mama, so we had nothin' ta buy one with. Ricky's daddy missed Ricky somethin' fierce. His mama still went 'round talkin' ta Ricky like he was there to listen, but his daddy knew better. Figured helpin' us was all he had left, helpin' us n' watchin' Ricky's baby grow up to look just like his daddy.

Ricky's daddy let me take his truck. Moonshinin' had a reputation back then. Most folks didn't mess with moonshiners, so even if they didn't approve, they kept their mouths shut. When I came pullin' up to our place in the woods, your daddy just nodded. Whatever morals he had left with your first night sleepin' on a empty stomach. Weren't much a man wouldn't do to feed his kid. Your mama wasn't happy, but she was hungry, so she just told us to be careful and don't build it too near where we was stayin'. Bein' as we'd spent most of our childhood in the woods, we knew where to go. Ingless was a little hole of a town south of us. Knew there was no law down there, and folks kept to themselves. We drove in, lights off, in the middle of the night and took the truck as far as we dared, not wantin' ta risk damage to the truck that weren't ours. Carried everything else in. Took all night; we just needed to get forty barrels of mash. That's what we'd heard was needed to get six barrels of shine. Some guys cut it with water, but we figured we had good equipment, we should use it to make good shine. In a rural area, folks remembered who sold 'em good shit, and who gave 'em gut rot. Weren't too hard to get that first load of mash. It was the right season and we knew lots of farmers. None of them wanted or needed to hire us, but weren't no problem findin' one of them willin' ta trust us with a load of mash on our word they'd get a cut of the first profits and some shine. Worked out an easy deal of us buyin' mash from then on.

We fell inta a routine pretty fast. Moved the still 'round every week or two, cleaned up everything after, so there weren't no proof we'd been there. We'd always been good at hidin' things in the woods. Weren't easy to move her round, even so. The pump made noise when it ran, so we had to keep her places where folks couldn't hear her runnin'. Even set up back where Josh and I had been out near Shellmound at one point, not too far from the train.

Lonny was still 'round town, and he was just the sorta guy you'd want to run a still with. Kept to himself and everyone was afraid of him. Well, he had a cousin was drivin' trains, mostly just to Gainesville and back. Made stops in just 'bout every town between Cedar Key and Gainesville, so we just kept close enough to get our gallons outta the trucks, and Lonny's cousin would stop and take us with 'em ta Gainesville where we'd sell 'em. Made a big profit once folks caught on how good our shine was. Josh helped us some. He'd gotten work cleanin' up the train stations. He'd keep a look out for us. Worked out a signal that let us know if it was safe to get off the train with our goods or if'n we needed to come back another day.

We had the mash and the train, but we also needed a hell of a lot of wood to keep the still runnin'. Fortunately, Ricky's daddy was always lookin' out. He and Olmos'd have me trimmin' trees and clearin' land all over the county. Billed me as some kinda handyman. I'd even hull the wood off myself. As long as the two of 'em got a small private supply, didn't mind none what I was doin' with the wood I hulled off. They lent us trucks when we needed 'em and asked no questions from us. If'n we ran outta mash, they'd connect me with where I could get some mash from one'a their uncles who had a big spread of land out by Bronson.

Well, that was the start of our business. Ran it that way for years—one step ahead of the Feds the whole time. Josh watched at the train stop in Gainesville, we had guys there waitin' ta buy when the coast was clear. Olmos' family got us the mash when our connections couldn't. Mil and I worked the still and Lonny's cousin ran the train. We did alright for ourselves for several years. Got to where at times you and your mama had a nice place in town and a car to get where you wanted to go. Course, sometimes we was stayin' out in the woods workin' without you two, but we was providin' for the family and that was the way things needed to be.

We had some close calls, but for the most part we was pretty safe runnin' the business. Like I said, weren't no one tellin' on us in that small town. We was intimidatin', and we shared with those who weren't dry and scared. There was one close call. I remember it was a stormy night. Me and your daddy was stayin' out at the still that weekend, all hiked up inta the woods, just off of Cedar Key; we was workin' on movin' on to the next place, but for that night we was just sittin' and relaxin'. We was on some of the land left open just off of the coast. We weren't drinkin' that night. Much as I liked to drink, and I knew our stuff was good, your daddy wasn't drinkin' much just then and I wasn't drinkin' alone much right then. Well, it was stormin' somethin' fierce. We had sat and watched the storm rollin' in offa the water. Started with the waves pickin' up, white caps comin' where there weren't normally any waves. We sat in our little shack, fire lit, just watchin' the waves. We was safe and dry, and we always liked watchin' a good storm. The wind picked up and near put out our fire, but we'd planned the shack right to keep us dry and safe, assumin' the storm weren't too big. Weren't the right season for a hurricane, so we relaxed, talked and watched it roll in. The thunder was startin' ta peel like big drums up in the sky, but the lightin' was winnin' that battle. It was one zap after another, just a lightin' up the sky. Guess that's what gave' em away. The sky lit up just as I turned around and I saw somethin' movin' out towards the road. We was situated just right, down by the water; we could see the one way in and out, but we had ourselves a different way that weren't known by none but locals. Well, I saw movement and knew weren't nobody out in that storm unless they was huntin' shiners. I nudged Mil and stood up, and that's all it took. We grabbed the last few pieces of equipment. Had to leave a few barrels of shine, but that was always a risk. Weren't nothin' ta tie our names to those barrels. The heavy equipment had already been put in the truck, fortunately. It was like God was watchin' out for us, makin' sure we didn't lose too much of our stuff. Felt like he was on our side, anyways.

Those Feds, they didn't know who they was takin' on. We knew those woods, and we was prepared to sneak out on a moment's notice, and we did. Left on foot and was takin' off in our truck by the time they got themselves to what was left of our camp. I imagine it made them pretty mad, seein' as we left the fire burinin' in the makeshift shelter we'd built, and our cups of hot coffee sittin' on stumps by the fire. They knew they just missed us, but they had no way of catchin' us and no way of knowin' who they'd missed. We had a few close calls, but that one was the closest. Weren't enough to worry us none. We was fairly safe, we was makin' money, and you and your mama was fed and warm.

Life went on nice like that. I hope you remember when life was good and we was happy. We had each other and we had food which was more'n most folks had then. It all ended in '32 when Lonny finally lost his cool. Shoulda known not to go inta business with such a hot head. Well, he got to drinkin' and to braggin'. Eventually, his braggin' led the Feds to the still when it was his night to keep watch. Lonny weren't the type to go down without a fight and I suppose he didn't that night. But seein' as the Feds shot him in the back, it's hard to be sure he had the chance to defend hisself. We lost less than Lenny that day to be sure, but we did lose our jobs again. Wasn't no easy way of findin' jobs then, and it didn't take long before we lost the house and the car. That's what led us up to DC with Josh and so many other Vets. But let me back up a bit.

CHAPTER TWENTY

Happiness

Your mama'd been wantin' a baby somethin' fierce. Back before Rosewood, she'd been losin' babies and the loss was hittin' her hard. Josh's mom'd stepped in. Josh'd brought his mama to the house after another little one was lost, and she sat out on the porch talkin' ta your mama for hours. Made her some tea and they just sat there sippin' and chattin'. I'd like to say she never lost a baby after that but turned out she was already pregnant again at that point. That was the last one she lost right after Rosewood. Then she did what Josh's mom had said, and she never lost another baby again, 'least not before birth.

Your daddy told me later that Josh's mama explained some kinda calendar method of avoidin' makin' babies. T'weren't really somethin' that concerned me so I can't explain it to you, but your daddy was willin' ta do anything to help your mama, so he followed whatever rules your mama passed on from Josh's mama. Apparently, she needed time to let her body heal from the loses, maybe more than most women did. She kept herself from gettin' pregnant for a spell after that and when enough time had passed, she followed the herbal regiment Josh's mama had left her to help her body keep the baby. Not sure if it was the herbs or just your mama lettin' her body have a few years to heal, but that baby made his way into the world.

We was still moonshinin' then, so your mama had lots of food and rest, but when the time came for the baby to be born, we was spendin' the weekend out in the woods. The little guy came early and surprised us all.

The problem was, there weren't no doctors round there and Josh's family'd been gone for years. Your mama had made a plan though. Woman always had a plan and a few back up plans. There was an old lady nearby. She scared me. She kept her hair piled up all messy like on her head, but off to the side, with bits of grey, straw-like, white hair hangin' out. Her eyes was glazed over and it seemed as she was never really lookin' at you, but lookin' beyond you to somethin' you couldn't quite see.

Didn't matter to me none. You and your mama liked her. She gave you some of her potato candy every time you saw her, so of course you liked her. What was important was that she knew how to birth a baby, and your mama had done this once before with you. Your mama sent you to get us, and your daddy sent me to get the creepy lady when the time came, and she weren't concerned none. Thought it weren't too awful early. She told me and Mil to stay outside and we didn't argue none. We sat on the front stoop sippin' some of the shine to help with the screams we was hearin' from inside the house. You came out once to get some. Said the old lady wanted some to clean with. Not sure she did clean up your mama with it, or if she just drank it herself, but no matter. She got you and your mama through it all and soon enough we heard a baby cryin'. Brought tears to your daddy's eyes. He sat there next to me cryin' and waitin' ta be called in. Truth be told, we both shed some tears that day. It was a long time comin', waitin' on one of your siblings to make their way inta the world. Your daddy had started worryin' the gas had done somethin' ta him he didn't know 'bout, somethin' that made him unable to make babies that could live, somethin' that affected his seed. This showed he was okay, and they could have more babies. Boy, did he love your brother. When he finally got let in the room with your mama, he said your brother was the most beautiful baby boy. Looked a lot like a hairy, little, red-faced thing to me. Had a head full'a black hair, and your mama was so proud. Even when the still got shut down, she was so happy to be a mama to a baby again, she didn't care none. That little man brought life back inta the family. He breathed, and often screamed, joy. Even as young as you was, you never once complained 'bout needin' ta help. You'd change and clean him and sing the whole time. You'd sway over him, with your brown hair swingin' over his chubby, little face, just as happy as you could be. Most'a the time you'd make up your own songs, and he'd coo right along with you, but even if he was screamin', you didn't mind none.

Your mama told me once that her empty arms had been achin' for the babies she lost and now the ache was gone. Her arms were full, and she'd been comforted.

Before the baby came, your mama'd found distraction workin' with Rosie at Green Shudders, sometimes stayin' the night after, other times Rosie and her son would stay at our house in town, while we was out deliverin' shine or movin' the still. Sometimes you'd work, too. You liked bein' able to help put money inta the house, even when it wasn't needed so much. Well, workin' gave your mama distraction, she told me, and she loved that she got to work with you. The men in town loved comin' inta see you there. Most of them knew us when we was your size, either cuz they went to school with us or cuz their kids did, and seein' you brought them back more and more, 'long with your mama's smile and Rosie's cookin'.

As much as she loved bein' at Green Shudders, like it was some kinda second home, havin' a baby again brought fulfillment and contentment in a deeper way to both of you. Rosie had to hire help to replace you for a time, 'til things got hard and work slowed for her. Of course, the bad comes in groups, as bad things often do, and the still was taken not long after the baby came and Rosie wasn't needin' help so much anymore. That left us without a lot of options, and so we was finally ready to hear Josh out about the Bonus Army. They was marchin' on DC and tryin' to get a better life for all of us that had came back from the war. We hadn't wanted to go all the way up to DC; we liked livin' in Levy, but now we needed money and we had no way left to make it. It was time for a change, and time to fight for a break.

CHAPTER TWENTY-ONE

The Bonus Army: Darkness in the Capital

It's time to talk about the worst time—what really did your daddy in. You know this part, but maybe there are things you don't know. Like I said, we couldn't get no work after the Feds closed in on our moonshinin' business. Things were bad in town at the time. Josh had been buggin' us to join up with the group callin' themselves the Bonus Army in DC. Guys were marchin' on the capital demanding payment from the government—money we'd been promised. Your daddy and me finally reached the point where we was willin' ta join Josh and the other guys and make our way up to DC. Your daddy, Josh, and I pooled what we had left from moonshinin' ta get you, your mama, and the baby train tickets for the trip. We didn't have enough to get everyone up there on a train, seein' as how we wanted to have some money when we got there to set up before we found jobs. Your daddy planned on train hoppin' up there with me and Josh, but we wouldn't let him. Didn't want to see the three of you ridin' up on your own. Weren't safe. We insisted he used more of the money to escort you three up there.

Josh wasn't allowed on trains, at least not in the normal sittin' sections, and I wasn't goin' without him. So, we was hoppin' from train to train to get up there. Y'all made it up there faster than we did, but boy, did we have a time. We weren't in no particular hurry to make our way up there, and we was two guys on our own with no responsibilities or worries. We stopped at a few spots along the way and camped out for a night or two. Found a good spot in South Carolina we both liked. Lots of good fishin' there and not too many folks around. We ate what we could catch, and we also had some food from the cans and cookies your mama packed us. Rosie gave me two loaves of her homemade bread, too. Told me to give 'em hell in Washington when we got there.

Well, we thought we would do just that. After all, weren't right that we'd been paid a dollar a day when our lives was on the line. The country'd been arguin' 'bout givin' us our due for some time, but they hadn't come to no agreement yet, and

we was all havin' a hard time gettin' on what with the way
the economy was with the depression and all. The government
had paid businesses they felt were owed money for war efforts.
But we weren't worth the country's money. After all, it was
the 1930s, and we weren't gonna wait for the money was due
us any longer. Congress'd been arguing over whether or not to
give us a bonus for our blood, sweat, tears and limbs lost for
long enough. The argument seemed to have settled on givin'
us some kind of bonus in several years. Some of the guys was
able to get loans based on that promise and they set up shops
or bought farms. Not us. Levy county banks had been all but
destroyed in the stock market crash. They didn't have that kind
of capital. After the moonshinin', your daddy tried to get a
loan out of Alachua county. Folks there had a lot more money,
but no. All they knew about us was what they'd read in the
papers, even if the papers was just speculatin'. They weren't
fixin' ta help no n- - - -r lovin', moonshinin' vets. Even if there
was no proof, the papers always liked to speculate on who
it was the Feds was tryin' ta catch, and the Feds was happy
to run our names through the mud, seein' as they couldn't
catch us. So, when Josh brought up this Bonus Army again, we
signed right up, so to speak. Your mama was happy we might
find a way to set ourselves up legitimate like. For me and Josh,
it seemed like another adventure, somethin' ta do, and maybe
we would get the money was owed us.

When we got to DC, your daddy had set up a tent with
room for me and Josh. We'd wanted y'all to have privacy, but
your daddy said some of the guys in the Hooverville weren't

safe to be around you and your mama. We worked together so you girls would never be alone. There was a guy next tent over who served with your daddy under Patton. I didn't know this for years after, but they was the only two left standin' at the end of Patton's uphill charge. They'd pulled Patton to safety at one point in the night. Shoulda left him to die. But now I'm gettin' ahead of myself again.

This fella, can't right remember his name, he was a real skinny guy. He'd left a job payin' decent money to make a dollar a day to serve his country in the war. When he came back, the job was gone and no one was hirin' vets, particularly not vets who twitch a lot and don't sleep at night. Well, this fella, he walked all the way from New Jersey to DC. Didn't even hop no trains, just walked. Figured he'd been robbed enough, and he wasn't gonna rob the train by takin' a ride for free. Guy was somethin' else. Figured he'd make a good neighbor, and he did help look out for ya'll, but there was enough guys there sufferin' and drinkin', he was right to keep an eye out for your safety, I suppose, though that weren't a problem in the end.

We all got lookin' for work right quick. Your daddy and I found work in some fancy restaurants cookin'. Turns out not everyone in DC knew how to skin and cook fish or what to do with oysters, so they hired us. Things were good then. It wasn't steady work. They already had steady guys, but we'd get to work on the weekends when they was busy, always leavin' one of us at home in the tent with y'all. When it was your daddy's turn to be home, he'd take you to the library. It was a long walk, and we didn't have no money for rides. Once you was there, he'd read to you for hours. He told me your favorite was *Frankenstein*. Your mama thought it was too much for a young girl, but you told me it reminded you of me and your daddy. Said the government had made me and your daddy and then left us. Didn't want its creatures when we didn't turn out as planned or when we weren't needed no more. Wouldn't give us a hope at a life or some sort of created happiness with our bonus but denied us just as Victor denied his creature the chance at a separate but happy life. Big thoughts for a little lady, but you was always like that. Took after your daddy in that way.

You and I didn't read much together. That was a lot of sittin' still for me at that point. Although I am sittin' and thinkin' a lot now—I wasn't then. You and I would walk with your mama and the baby down to the Potomac. A lot of the guys from camp couldn't catch fish outta the river to save their lives, but I was a Levy boy. I knew how to make a cane pole and catch a fish with my eyes closed. That's where I taught you to do the same. Your mama weren't much for fishin', but she liked the chance to get out from the camp and sit by the river for a while, and she liked watchin' you catch fish and laugh with me at the rich folks walkin' by. You weren't never jealous of what they had, just liked laughin' at their silly hats and their silly ways of walkin' with their babies in fancy proms and such.

And so we made it, little by little. Between the warehouse work we could get, the cookin', eatin', and tradin' fish we caught with that fella in the tent next to us, well, we did alright. Weren't movin' outta the tent no time soon, but we was alright and bein' with the guys in the Hooverville was like bein' home again. Josh and I would walk into DC with guys from camp when your daddy was home, and there weren't much work to be found, which happened sometimes, and we'd walk in and sit on the lawn in the mall in downtown DC and just watch the swells go by in their suits. Sometimes, we'd sit right on the lawn and laugh at them, like me and you used to do, but maybe a bit less kind than you were. That's where we met the guy in the green hat. Now that guy was a guy who knew how to work a angle. I don't know where to start with this guy. When we're young, we have this innocent trust of those in charge. We end up trustin' politicians for a time. They're off in a separate world almost, doin' right and leadin' us. Or so it seems, unless the adults near you say differently. This bubble had been burstin' for me for some time—really since the war. Whatever was left of it burst when I met this guy in the green hat. You see, Mil and me had been runnin' that still. Gettin' busted by the Feds broke us financially. We knew we was breakin' the law, but we was hopin' ta get away with it to provide for ourselves and for you and your mama. Gettin' busted led to us goin' to DC. We couldn't see no other way to make ends meet. The economy was trashed. No one was hirin', no one was loanin'. Then we met this man in the green hat. This guy was sellin' alcohol to the swells on Capitol Hill, and everyone knew it. They even gave him a office so he could sell to Congress in private more easily. These bastards voted for Prohibition and then brought in the man in the green hat to sell them alcohol privately. Word has it the Feds fed him information on where to find the best stuff because they wanted to buy some of it. They was bustin' the little guys like us out in the sticks, and then they was feedin' information to this guy in the workplace so they might could get some of the good stuff themselves.

He seemed like a nice enough guy. Couldn't blame him for takin' advantage of a situation that put food on his table. He offered Josh and me jobs when we met him, but we turned him down on principle. Weren't right. Told your dad about it, and he didn't want the job neither. Far as I know that was the only job offer your dad ever did turn down. He was desperate to feed and clothe y'all better. Felt your mama deserved more, but that job was too risky, he said. When we was busted in Levy County, we was able to hide. Everyone knew it was us, but no one in the law could prove it was us. That was a small risk. Mil was afraid of federal prison time. Turns out, that woulda been the better risk.

CHAPTER TWENTY-TWO

Patton

Your daddy was so careful 'bout never leavin' you kids and your mama alone in the camp. He didn't trust all the guys in the camp, and he was always afraid for your safety with all those hungry men 'round. But it wasn't the men he shoulda been afraid of. They was his fellow soldiers. They had his back. Always did. It was the brass he shoulda been worryin' 'bout. We knew President Hoover wasn't happy we was there. That was kinda the point. If we camped in the park, in our own little Hoovervilles, maybe they'd give us our bonus. We was pretty happy. We worked. We talked. Life was good, but not for Hoover, you see. Didn't look good for the president to have vets campin' out on the front steps in DC. He needed us to go, and payin' us wasn't somethin' he was interested in doin'.

We'd gotten word he was callin' in the big dogs to clear us out. Rumor was Patton would be the one to get us all out. Well, we figured this was good news. Patton was brass, but he was one of us. Your daddy had served with Patton in France. If it wasn't for your daddy, Patton wouldn't even be alive. Your daddy saved his ass. If he'd'a known how things would play out, he woulda let that piece of shit die in the forest. Let the Krauts take him out.

But we don't get to see ahead in life. That day when we heard Patton was comin', your daddy went out to find him. The guys all knew the story of your daddy savin' Patton. He was kinda famous 'mong them for that. They thought he could make some kind of bargain with Patton, get him to see things our way, or at least get him to help us clear out safely if it came to that. Your daddy's plan was always to make it better for you and your mama, and for all us guys, but he couldn't even get to Patton that day. Wouldn't see your daddy. Closest he got was Eisenhower, MacArthur's aide-de-camp. Eisenhower wouldn't even bring a message to Patton or MacArthur. Said MacArthur saw the Bonus Army as a serious test of the strength of the government and they wouldn't back down. One of the guys had served with MacArthur, too. He tried to get directly to MacArthur, but he was leadin' the calvary and they couldn't get nowhere near him. All that huntin' 'round tryin' ta get near Patton or MacArthur put us at the back side of what we shoulda seen as a hostile army.

Well, those guys, they took their calvary and tanks under MacArthur and Patton and led them right inta our camp. We was unarmed and didn't stand a chance. Your mama, she'd laid down to nap with the baby before it all started. Didn't know what was comin'. "Sleep when the baby sleeps" people always said. Still do. She didn't see the danger comin', bein' in the middle of the camp as she was. Your mama, once she was sleepin', was difficult to wake up. You and your daddy always had to wake her when the baby cried. "She slept like a rock," your daddy always said. "Can't wake that woman once she gets to sleepin'." It shouldn't'a cost her what it did. You was readin' one of your library books beside your mama when Patton charged in. You were so young and used to the noise of camp, didn't think much of it at first, and it happened so fast. By the time you realized those were shots you was hearin', the calvary was on top of you. Tanks, too. They ran right over the tents, which weren't built to last anyways. The roof of our tent collapsed on the side of the tent your baby brother was sleepin' in. By the time you and your mama got up, it was too late. Couldn't even get the baby out. The walls of the tent were made outta whatever we could find and was set up with makeshift furniture and such. Couldn't get the baby out from under it all, and there was tanks there holdin' stuff in place. Weren't much time anyway. Patton's men were draggin' your mama out howlin' and hittin'. Tied her arms up like she was under arrest and left her under guard with some of the others didn't want to leave. That's where we found you both. There's nothin' like the loss of a child. Your daddy knew when he saw your mama without her sayin' nothin'. He just fell on the ground howlin'. When he started screamin' your brother's name, I knew. It was like the earth gave way under me, and all I could hear was screamin'. Took a few minutes to realize it was me screamin'. Three of us couldn't stop shakin' for hours. Just sat there on the side of the road where they'd put your mama, just sat there cryin'. Some newspaper guys came 'round and took pictures and wrote about it, I guess. I heard later, anyways. Don't remember much from that time. Doc said we was in shock, and I guess he was right. Nothin' prepares you for the death of a child. Boy wasn't even two. My mind couldn't wrap itself around him bein' gone. Kept expectin' him to come 'round the corner just a grinin'.

The three of us couldn't do much for you that day. Don't know how much of this you remember. You wasn't that old, and the mind tends to let go of what it can't handle. Well, Josh, he was the one to keep an eye on you. When we was all sobbin', he walked over, found you sittin' behind a bush, just picked you up and cradled you in his arms like you was a baby. He told me later you felt it was your fault. You shoulda heard 'em comin' and gotten the baby or waked your mama up. You shoulda seen the danger a-comin'. I never brought myself to talk to you about it. It's so hard for me to talk about it, and it's easier to try and forget. I need you to know, it wasn't your fault, or your mama's fault. Your daddy and I blamed ourselves, but the truth is it weren't our fault neither. This is on the shoulders of Patton, MacArthur, Hoover, Eisenhower and their men. They did this. Two vets were killed that day by United States soldiers on US soil. They was unarmed. Two babies were killed, including your brother. That was four families shattered. We couldn't even afford a funeral. That day destroyed us, and truth be told, there weren't no way comin' back from this blow.

Way your daddy saw it, Patton deserved to die for what he did. Your daddy kept readin' me this poem by Kipling. Halal had made us memorize it as kids in school. Well, he told us to anyways. Me and the guys cheated, but you know how your daddy was. He loved poetry. Found solace in it, even to the end. He memorized that poem and never forgot it. He told me once that poetry helped him through battles, especially in the moments he was most afraid. He would start thinkin' through poems he'd memorized and just keep movin' forward. Sometimes he'd even recite 'em out loud while he was walkin'. That's what he did when he risked his own life to save Patton. Anyways, the verse I remember your daddy sayin' the most went somethin' like this:

They are hangin' Danny Deever, you must march 'im to 'is place
For 'e shot a comrade sleepin', you must look 'im in the face;
Nine 'undred of 'is country, an' the regiment's disgrace,
While they're hangin' Danny Denver in the mornin'

Guess he liked to think on a guy dyin' for killin' a soldier on his side of the game. Your daddy figured Patton deserved to hang for what he'd done—killin' US vets on US soil, just like Deever did for shootin' a comrade. All of 'em deserved it. T'weren't what happened, though. That's never what happened with brass when they done wrong. Patton, as you know, he's been glorified, and we was cast out. We wasn't worth the nation's money or help. After your daddy lost his left arm and got his face all disfigured servin' the nation, they didn't need him no more. He was used up and tossed out.

Only one to pay, as it turned out, was Hoover. FDR came out puttin' down what had been done. Most folks agreed. Didn't want to help us, but they weren't for killin' us or our children, neither. So, it cost Hoover his reelection, but I suppose the economy woulda done that anyways. FDR weren't much better.

Your daddy never got over this part of his story. Blamed himself for what happened 'til the day he died. Turned to drinkin' more heavily. Couldn't be there for your mama. Neither could I. Truth is, it destroyed us all, and we just kept movin' forward cuz we had to.

CHAPTER TWENTY-THREE

Regret

This. This is the part I've been dreadin' tellin' you 'bout. Your father was the best man I have ever known. When I lost him, I lost half of myself. You've asked me why he left. You, like the government, worry he isn't really dead, but I've been writing this to show you he is. You may have trouble puttin' together the man you remember with the man I've been tellin' you 'bout, but you see, war breaks all of us, and we never really heal. In the beginning, he was so happy to be alive, so happy to be home with you and your mama. I turned to drink when I came back. Well, that's not entirely true. I never turned away from drink, so I never turned back to it, neither. I've been this way since the Italian Front. But not your daddy. He made it through without drinkin' too much and without women. He ran home to you and your mama. Eventually, the nightmares caught up with him. The dead would visit him in the night. He'd see those we lost and those he killed. At times, he thought death itself was stalkin' him, as if he'd gotten away when he shouldn't've. This led to him not sleepin'. If he wasn't asleep, he didn't see 'em—at first. Then he kept gettin' flashbacks. Loud noises frightened him. He started drinkin' more to wash all of that away, and it helped for a while, but his fear and anger broke through. He started gettin' violent.

Your mama came to me at this point. Josh and I tried to help, but I suppose we was too broken to be of much good, and besides, 'round us he wasn't violent, but the nightmares came and he didn't like that. He was a sensitive soul. Never shoulda gone to France, and that—that was my fault. I was goin' and thought he should go with me. I shoulda seen he needed to stay home, shoulda gone to school or somethin'. He coulda used marryin' your mama to put off the draft. Didn't need to volunteer. I shouldn't of pushed him.

I say he got violent, but maybe that's not the best way to say it. Now he never hit your mama and you, but I'm guessin' you remember how angry he got as you weren't young then, that's what I mean by violent. He got angry—broke things, yelled some. He tried to keep it under control, but then if anger isn't dealt with, it sorta bubbles up when you least expect it, and that is how your mama lost her finger—and that is why your daddy left.

I think your mama told you she was cuttin' carrots and accidentally cut it off, but that wasn't the case. Your daddy had been drinkin'. The roof was leakin' and money was tight. We were back in Levy then, but he'd never been the same since your brother died. I guess he went out after drinkin' a bunch. Not sure how much he'd had, but I'm guessin' it was a lot. Went to the sawmill. Guy who ran the sawmill was lettin' your daddy saw a few boards off free of charge to fix the roof for you and your mama. Guy knew your daddy was in a spot, but he didn't know your daddy was heavy in drink. It was after hours, so your daddy had the place to hisself and your mama knew he'd gone in drunk. She worried about him hurtin' hisself, so she went down to find him. I guess she startled him workin' bein' as he wasn't in his clear mind. I figured afterwards, he'd had at least six beers before she'd gotten there and he was still drinkin'. Well, when she came up behind him, he started and shoved her off and your mama's hand fell inta the saw blade. Her right little finger came clear off. Blood was everywhere when I got there, but your mama wasn't even cryin'. She was just sittin' with her hand wrapped up, tryin' ta calm your daddy down, rubbin' his back and tellin' him it was goin' ta be okay. The law didn't bring no charges against your daddy, and they didn't need to. He lost his mind over hurtin' your mama, and he knew he couldn't let the nightmares and the drink lead to him hurtin' your mama again. He had to get right in the head and make things better for you and your mama again, somehow.

'Bout that time, Josh and me'd been buggin' him to go to one of those CCC camps with us. He hadn't wanted to go because he wanted to be with his family, but he knew then what he had to do. He told me he was gonna leave you and work with me in one of them Keys camps so he could work on not drinkin' and gettin' hisself right in the head. Said he'd send money home to your mama. For her part, she didn't want him to go, but she knew that it was right. But as a little girl, you didn't see how it was. I remember the day we pulled away from Gainesville headed for the Keys. Josh, he'd stayed in Gainesville as the work camp for blacks was separate in the area and not in the Keys. Boy, you cried and yelled at your mama when the train pulled out. Josh tried to help your mama calm you. Broke your daddy's heart to leave you wailin' on the train platform, but also made him more determined to get back to you both—fully back and not just the broken shell he had been. Didn't say a word through the whole train ride. He just sat and thought. He was determined.

CHAPTER TWENTY-FOUR

The Keys

Camp life wasn't so bad. We got there in the dark, and that mornin', watchin' the sun rise up in the east over that clear, blue water was a healin' sensation I'll never forget. Course, we'd been travelin' for a bit in a sweaty old train full of guys headin' to work and not so concerned with cleanin' themselves—really made that fresh ocean breeze feel like a miracle when we got off at our stop. Couldn't wait to go fishin'. I'd heard there was some real good fishin' off those shores. That first mornin', the tide was out real low like. Almost looked like we could walk to another island; some of the guys from up North talked about it, but we knew what that muddy sand was like after the tide and we wouldn't let 'em. Figured we'd have to wait a bit to fish since we didn't have no boats.

Tide came in eventually, and it did not disappoint. We had the first day to explore the beaches and the town and to get ourselves settled. Didn't figure I had much to settle in with, seein' as I had the clothes on my back, an extra pair of clothes in my sack, and my fishin' gear I was fixin' to use, so I had planned on spendin' most of my time fishin' in those clear waters once the tide came in. Most of the guys was headin' inta town, and I'd had about enough time with them on the train, so fishin' seemed the way to go. Stripped down to just our pants, me and your daddy did, and we pulled those up above our knees and waded out as far as we could. Water was waist deep so not sure why we hiked our pant legs up, but it's just one of those things you do. Didn't have much luck at first, but we did have fun. We was laughin' and enjoyin' the time off we had in the water. Eventually, the fish did come, as they usually did. Me and your daddy knew 'bout what kind of bait to use and where to cast. Brought in a bunch of keepers that night. Not enough to feed the army that was campin' and waitin' ta start work the next day, but enough to win us some friends. Guys was willin' ta trade all sorts of things to get in on the fish fry we was cookin' round the fire that night. That made up for only comin' down with fishin' gear and two sets of clothes. Started buildin' up some bedding, and of course your daddy took any books he was offered. Even took some book written by a Vanderbilt on the proper etiquette for a woman. Not sure what he wanted that for, you was always gonna be more of a fishin' and huntin' kinda girl, like Rosie, but he musta figured your mama would be happy to have you have it, so he traded some fish for that book our first night, thinkin' he might could mail it to you or bring it when we was done. I just shook my head. Fish was worth more than that.

Suppose I should tell you 'bout how we was livin' in the Keys. We was boardin' in these wooden huts outside'a town and right on the water. At high tide, the water was nearly to the huts and sometimes high tide could put the campfires out, but the huts kept us pretty dry, unless the wind was blowin' the rain just right and then we got soaked. Guys that got there before us told us those was recently built. Before then, they was in tents and had no bathrooms. Bathrooms was still lackin', but it reminded me of livin' out on Shellmound with Josh. We didn't care none for the most part. We worked hard by day, real physical labor, and then we had the night to set 'round the fire with the other guys. All of us had been overseas somewhere, and all of us had seen somethin' worth forgettin'. Some of the guys would spend their money on alcohol and drink it 'round the fire, but your daddy was focused on gettin' clean and I figured I outta help him, so neither of us was drinkin'. No one questioned, we just sat around tradin' jokes and stories. Course, most of the stories was the sort soldiers like to tell, not the kind of stories that maybe they need to tell. They talked a lot about girls they met, or said they met, but that all sounds the same after a while. One guy, he'd served up in France somewheres, not near your daddy, but I can't right remember where. Anyways, this guy talked 'bout sneakin' out inta town to find some food for his unit. They wasn't on the front lines, so the danger wasn't great, but neither was the food. His NCO was a stiff sorta guy and didn't want no one goin' ta find better provisions, so he took it on hisself to do so. He got hisself all the way to the nearest town, fifty miles in one night to hear him tell it, and he found a French girl he claimed gave him five loaves of bread, an unlikely story. Said he'd given her a good time worth more than five loaves and that was her thankin' him. Soldiers like to talk that way when it's only them. Anyways, he said the loaves was so big he couldn't close his sack 'round 'em and had to leave them hangin outta the bag on his back. Well, guy said on his way back to his unit, he had to work 'round the long way to sneak back in 'round the guards on fire watch, and seein' as he hadn't been that way before, he didn't know the terrain. When he was walkin' in the dark usin' the stars to guide him, a dog came outta nowhere and took a loaf. Well, he still had four, but he wanted all five. He figured he could sell 'em back to the rest of his unit. Real nice guy, this guy. So, he went after the dog, only the dog knew what it was doin' and ran him inta a barn where two other dogs was waitin'. Said it was an ambush, and in the end he had no bread and in chasin' 'em he ran through some mud and lost a boot. Not only did he come back empty-handed, but he came back hungry, tired, and down a boot. NCO wasn't havin' none of it or his story. Put him on latrine duty for a week. Most of the guys listenin' ta that story figured he was out gamblin' and that was the best story he could come up with to cover it, but it was funny to hear him tell it. That's the way it was. Guys sittin' 'round tellin' stories that might or might not be true. That same guy told stories most nights, and we liked hearin' him talk, but we didn't buy much of what he said. One time he was up tellin' us all about how he used to drive cattle. Now, lots of guys we knew got inta drivin' cattle for rich folk in central Florida, so we knew a bit about it, though we never really did that kinda work ourselves. Well, he got to braggin' bout how handy he was with a whip and one of the guys wanted him to demonstrate. Guy got up in front of everyone and got a horse whip from his tent. Can't for the life of me think of why he brought that with him to the Keys. Said he was gettin' back to cattle when the CCC work dried up, but like I said, we didn't believe nothin' that guy said. So, he stands up and starts whippin' that thing 'round. Everyone gives him his space 'cuz we was well aware of how much one of those things would hurt, thanks to our daddy. Well, he's whippin' it 'round, five or six beers in, and he hits hisself in the left side of his face, only that whip done wrapped 'round his face and caught him on the other side of the face. Funniest thing I'd seen in a long while. We didn't let him live that one down for some time, then again, neither did the bruises on his face.

Most nights went that way. Your daddy and me sat around the fire, sippin' sweet tea and talkin', listenin' ta the guys tell their stories. Some of 'em got funnier the more they drank. Your daddy didn't need the drink. Just bein' with other vets brought somethin' out in your daddy, brought him back to his story tellin' days. He started writin' and rememberin' poetry. Reminded me of the old Mil. There was even a camp newspaper he and another guy put together to share with all the Keys camps. The other guy, he had been an artist before the war and he started drawin' pictures for Mil's stories. Hadn't drawn in years. Somethin' about bein' all together, all of us against the world, workin' hard for our food—real honest work. Brought healin' and real honest-ta-goodness laughter. I hadn't heard your daddy laugh in a while. It was good to hear him cuttin' up every night, and I wish you coulda seen him. He was stashin' money aside for you all, not wastin' it on nothin', not even eatin' nice, and he was workin' his way back to you. He could see his way home.

One of the townsfolk had a private library and a heart for us vets. Think his son didn't find his way home, and neither did his body, so he was kind to us guys. Not all the folks felt that way, seein' as we was a noisy and smelly sorta group. Well, this guy took a likin' to your daddy and would let him borrow books. Some nights, Mil would read to all of us. Not all the guys could read, and they liked the way your daddy would read. He was like when he read to you and your baby brother, got all animated like and made different accents for the different characters, givin' 'em lisps and even walkin' around with a hunch in his back when he read that Hugo book 'bout the church. Made the guys laugh. What he loved to read them most was poetry, his poetry and the poetry other soldiers had written. Course some of it was banned, so we was fortunate this guy in town wasn't the sort to let a government ban stop him from gettin' a book he knew he and Mil would like. This one was wrote by some guy named Owen who didn't come back from the war; it's one Mil read a lot and the guys took a real shine to it:

> After the blast of lightning to the east,
> The flourish of loud clouds, the Chariot Throne,
> After the drums of time have rolled and ceased,
> And by the bronze west long retreat is blown,
> Shall life renew these bodies? Of a truth
> All death will he annul? All tears assuage?
> Or fill these void veins full again with youth,
> And wash, with an immortal water, Age?
> When I do ask white Age he saith not so:
> "My head hangs weighed with snow."
> And when I hearken to the Earth, she saith:
> "My fiery heart shrinks, aching.
> It is death.
> Mine ancient scars shall
> not be glorified,
> Nor my titanic tears, the seas, be dried."

Didn't seem to offer a lot of hope that one, but it's funny how hearin' your thoughts written on a page by some other guy can bring hope and rest. That's what we was gettin', even more so than when we was in DC. In DC, we was waitin' on hope and wantin' work, here we had work. Didn't have you and your mama, but your daddy knew he was gettin' there.

One night, we was sittin' 'round the fire pit, only bein' as it was summer, weren't no fire. We was just sittin' and enjoyin' the breeze and the company. The ocean was real still like, and it reflected every light in the area like a black mirror. The moon could look down on its cousin in the water, and we could see every light in town, not that there were many then. The peacefulness of the water kinda laid us all back and got us thinkin' more than usual. One of the guys got to talkin' 'bout this group of French soldiers. Guys were stuck in one line of trenches for years and they weren't makin' no progress. The men in charge, who never were the ones takin' the risks, kept sendin' 'em over the top, and they could never make any ground. The Germans were entrenched and weren't goin' nowhere. These frogs got tired of not gettin' nowhere, and they refused to go anymore. A protest of sorts. They weren't leavin', they weren't backin' down, they just weren't goin' over the top no more. Guy said he heard it from this Frenchman when he was on leave after the fightin' stopped. Wrote a song 'mong themselves to tell why they wasn't goin' over the top no more. The French frog told him that the Frenchies offered one million Francs and immediate honorable discharge to the guy who would turn in the author of this song, and no one would talk. A free trip home and money enough for five lifetimes, and guys still wouldn't rat out the unit that wrote this song of protest. This frog said he was one of five hundred guys condemned to death because of the song, although not even one of ten of those guys was put down. Guess they figured they was probably gonna die anyways, might as well go out fightin' the government gettin' everyone killed.

Anyways, we all liked the idea of an illegal song, and we also liked hearin' it weren't just our government that was screwin' us over, so we all learned the song. Used to sing it round the campfire ring that summer. Went something like this:

When at the end of a week's leave,
We're going back to the trenches
Our place there is so useful that, without us,
We'd take a thrashing
But it's all over now, we've had it up to here,
Nobody wants to march anymore
And with hearts downcast, like when you're sobbing
We're saying goodbye to the civilians
Even if we don't get drums, even we don't get trumpets
We're leaving for up there with lowered head
Goodbye to life, Goodbye to love,
Goodbye to all the women
It's all over now, we've had it for good
With this awful war.
It is in Craonne, up on the plateau
That we're leaving our skins
'cause we've all been sentenced to die
We are the sacrifice
Eight days in the trenches, eight days of suffering
And yet we still have hope.
That tonight the relief will come
That we keep waiting for.

Suddenly, in the silent night, we hear someone approach
It's an infantry officer who's come to take over for us.
Quietly in the shadows, under a falling rain
The poor soldiers are going to look for their graves.
Goodbye to life, Goodbye to love,
Goodbye to all the women
It's all over now, we've had it for good with this awful war
It is in Craonne, up on the plateau
That we're leaving our skins
'cause we've all been sentenced to die
We are the sacrifice

On the grand boulevards it's hard to look
At all the rich and powerful whooping it up
For them life is good, but for us it's not the same
Instead of hiding, all these shirkers
Would do better to go up to the trenches
To defend what they have, because we have nothing
All of us poor wretches
All our comrades are being buried there
To defend the wealth of these men here.

Those who have the dough, they'll be coming back
Because it's for them that we're dying
But it's all over now because all of the grunts
Are going to go on strike
It'll be your turn,
All you rich and powerful gentlemen,

To go up onto the plateau.
And if you want to make war,
Then pay it with your own skins.

Sorta resonated with us, that one did. Course, we'd tried to strike up there in DC and it didn't get us nothin'. Those old fat sirs weren't goin' nowhere, and they wasn't gonna experience the way we was workin' no time soon.

CHAPTER TWENTY-FIVE

We are the Sacrifice

Anyways, we spent lots of time sittin' round the fire, but not all weekends and nights. Well, probably most of 'em were spent there for your daddy. Bein' as I didn't have a reason to put down drinkin' and fun, aside from your daddy, some weekends I went with the guys down to Key West and left him behind. That was gettin' on in the summer, and your daddy was doin' good by then. Hadn't drank in months. Felt like I could leave him and have some fun. The guys and I all took the train down to Key West on a Friday night, and we didn't plan on bein' back 'til the last train out. There were lots of hot spots for us to hit, and let me tell you, the sunset in Key West is better than any I seen anywhere else in Florida, and that's sayin' a lot for a Florida boy. I'd get a beer and sit on the edge of the main square, feet hangin' over the wall, and just watch the sun set like a gold ball droppin' inta the ocean. It was somethin' else.

'Course, not all my time in Key West was spent enjoyin' nature. Sure, I fished and swam, but I also did my share of bar hoppin' with the guys. There were some great bars down there, and we made the best of our time and our money. Saw friends of all kinds, but one that stands out the most is Hemingway. Guy got us. Had all the money in the world, from where I was sittin', but he had been where I had been, and he understood. Some of the people with money in the Keys were not happy with us. We made too much noise, and we drank too much. We was just an all-around nuisance. They wanted us gone, but we was of use to the government so we wasn't goin' nowhere. We was buildin' bridges and railroads, and like it or not, they needed us, in spite of our noise.

Anyways, Hemingway wasn't like that. Guy would sit and drink with us. Sometimes we'd take turns boxin' him. Everyone did. Not that he was all that good, it was more the novelty of it. Well, he had been to the part of Italy I had been in. He didn't remember meetin' me before, but he was always glad to meet another vet. We didn't know the same guys, as we was in different units, but we had been to some of the same towns. I had been to Kobarid. He hadn't, but he had put one of his characters in that area. Told me he'd been to the area,

162

but not to Kobarid. I let him know he got that part about the fountain wrong. Weren't no fountain at no time in that town. I don't think he liked bein' told he was wrong, but he was happy I'd read his book and liked it. Sorta liked knowin' other vets got what he had said. Bought us all a round of drinks. Gotta love a rich guy who buys drinks for you. We sure did have a time out with him. Made the trips to Key West even better. Anyways, turns out that wouldn't be the last time I saw Hemingway. This is the part I need you to sit down for, and it's more important than what your old Uncle Will did at bars in the Keys, so I will leave that story off and move on to the part you need to hear.

It's funny the things you remember, and the things you don't wanna remember. I can still hear the noise the hammers made. Guys were working twelve-hour shifts, bangin' away all day buildin' a railroad. Needed to be a railroad that stretched the length of Florida, all the way to the Keys, more than there needed to be quiet. Government weren't interested in the healin' we got from just bein' together. Weren't interested in much more than fixin' the economy and gettin' us off their lawn.

It was Labor Day weekend. Meant a lot to the guys cuz if they had the money, they could bus or train down to Key West and spend the long weekend at the bar. I tried not to go too often, and things didn't feel right to your daddy and I that weekend. The weather was off. We wasn't around when the last big hurricane came through our area at home, but we'd been told by all the old timers 'bout the storm of 1896. They made comparisons with that and every small storm that came through. Got to where feelin' the storms was in our blood, so to speak. Could see the calm in the waves, the humidity, kinda had a sense for it. The guys runnin' the camp wasn't from Florida. Didn't know and didn't listen none.

As the day went on, the weather was showin' her face a bit more. Tried talkin' ta the boss, but he weren't havin' none of us. They was sure we just wanted to get outta work; they wouldn't let none of us go, even though it was the weekend anyways and some of the guys had already left for Key West. Weren't no one else leavin' once we thought maybe there was a storm brewin'. Figured we just wanted to drink in Miami, I suppose. When we pushed, they pushed back. Took the keys to the trucks so we wouldn't be able to leave while they wasn't lookin'. Mil and I tried to figure a way to shore up camp a bit, but there weren't much we could do. Construction supplies were everywhere, waitin' ta become a part of the big railroad FDR was buildin'. The cabins weren't more than a few feet above the water at high tide as it was.

Thing was, the main boss was off in Key West with his wife that weekend. Weren't there to help make the decisions needed to be made. Messages weren't gettin from Key West to someone who would make a decision. Not sure anyone cared to anyway. Guys had been askin' all the way up to FDR for the Feds to build a hurricane shelter for us guys in the Keys for some time now, but the Feds said it was too much money. Thing was, FDR spent more than enough time in South Florida to know the danger these storms brought in. He knew when he said no that he could very well be damnin' those guys to their deaths.

No matter. There was no shelter. When the weather started to get real bad, they called in a train, wanted it to come and get us. Figured that was the way out, but it was too late. Wind started really pickin' up then. We was tryin' ta get the guys to shelter wherever they could find it—in the cabins or in a house in town, if someone would have 'em. Your daddy was out tryin' to convince guys to hunker down, but they didn't listen at first. Some of 'em managed to steal a truck, hot wire it, and get out. Heard later they washed away on the bridge. Truck was found, but they were among the missing after. Bodies weren't never found.

Guy who told all the stories was the one ended up convincin' the guys. He was out, screamin' inta the wind, wouldn't come inta the cabin for nothin'. See, by that time, it was dark outside. Couldn't see much, so he didn't see what was comin' for him. Big piece of wood, 2x4 by the looks of it, came flyin' at him. Truth be told, I didn't see it none until it went right through him. Guys started listenin' ta me and your daddy then, but there weren't much we could tell them. We had 'em all in cabins, but it weren't long before those started to come down, too.

'Bout that time the train came through, but it didn't do us much good. Storm turned it all on its side right away. What it did was give us a place to hide. After seein' the storm turn a train over, all crumbled and snake like, some of the guys didn't want nothin' ta do with it. Couldn't right talk to them as the storm was just a howlin'. Some of 'em took to tyin' themselves to trees. Figured the tree weren't goin' nowhere. Turns out that was right, but the wind brought so much water inta the air, most of those guys drowned tied to the tree, just tryin' ta breathe, even the ones who tied shirts round their faces. Didn't matter much. The wind took the clothes right off of their bodies, even the shirts tied round their faces.

Things weren't much better in the train, but it did keep the water from drownin' us—most of us. We sat in the dark, inside the belly of this box car and some of the guys were howlin' in fear. Not your daddy. He was brave. Started singin', though I'm not sure many guys could hear him. He was tryin' to calm 'em. Sang that French song, sang lullabies he'd sang you as a baby. Never was much of a singer, but he always put the needs of others first, and he knew those guys needed a distraction, even if he was competing with the wind to be heard.

When the eye came over, guys wanted to get outta there, but Mil and me knew that weren't no kind of idea. Bein' Florida boys, we knew the worst was still to come. Usually was with those sorta storms. A few of 'em tried to start swimmin' out to a boat they could see off-shore. Some of 'em started tryin' ta climb over stuff on the bridges to get out. None of 'em was seen again. A few of 'em made it inta town, I heard later. We decided the train had gotten us this far, we'd ride it out in there. We kept those with us that would listen, and we shored ourselves in, to sorta hunker down for what was to come.

When the wind picked up again, sounded like a freight train comin' through. Couldn't hear nothin', and Mil knew singin' weren't worth it. No one was hearin' nothin' for the rest of the storm. We linked arms, your daddy and I. If one of us was goin', so was the other. It was always like that with us.

About halfway through that part'a the storm, the wind or the water, hard to say which, picked up what looked like part of a house and busted open what was left of the window of that box car. The car was on its side, so the window was on top, and with nothin' holdin' out the wind and the rain, water came pourin' in. I'm a grown man, and I've faced much worse, but sittin' in that train, in the wind, the wet, and the dark, I was terrified. Didn't think I was gettin' outta that one alive. All of the men started linkin' arms at that point. We was like a chain of men, and the guys on the end were hangin' on to whatever seemed to be attached to the train. Your daddy was on one end and he'd gripped this bar attached to the wall of the train next to the door. Sort of thing guys grabbed to pull themselves inta the train. He had his whole arm worked through the bar and was white knuckle grippin' it, so to speak. Didn't have no hand to grip with but was grippin' with his elbow all the same.

The wind was relentless like. Didn't give up. Seemed like we was at the world's end, just waitin' ta fall off. Couldn't hear guys cryin' no more. We was just all holdin' on to each other for dear life. It weren't enough. Never is. The wind finally got those waves up and inta the window. Seemed like she'd been tryin' ta break in full force for hours. The water was so strong, washed your daddy right outta my left arm. In all my life, I have never been able to forget the feel of his arm slippin' from mine. Felt like slow motion, like a dance I couldn't stop. I tried to break free and swim after him, but the guy to my right wouldn't let go. Guy was huge. Had arms like a tree trunk. All I could do was flail in the water tryin' ta get out and grab your daddy. Turns out he was one of a few that washed out that night and all the rest of us could do was stay in the train and survive. My heart was broken in that moment, but my mind couldn't take it none. My mind was sure he was out there somewhere, in some tree or somethin'. Ain't no way no storm could take your daddy from me. We was one guy in two bodies. Kept hopin' he'd found a way. Your daddy always found a way. He'd make it. Find a tree or somethin'. For the rest of the storm, I sat there in the water at the end of those guys all linked together, takin' Mil's spot holdin' on to the bar and just waitin' for it to pass so I could go and find your daddy.

When the storm finally did pass, we was walkin' out inta a different world. Was worse than anything I ever saw after a battle had ended. There weren't nothin' left, just some trees, stripped of their leaves, leaves which'd been replaced with the bodies of some of the townspeople. Dead birds lay everywhere, and there were no sounds. Silence and death surrounded us as we crept outta the train, but still hope held on. We worked together, callin' for Mil and the other guys. Even the shore was different. Seemed odd. Such a small thing, too, but one of those thoughts that stayed with me for years after. The shore, the thing that was always there, the line between us and the ocean, was rearranged. Didn't matter none. We kept walkin' and callin' out. One of the guys, he had become childlike. Storm'd washed up bunches of shells. Some of 'em lived in, some of 'em not. Somethin' broke in this guy and he just walked the shore, talkin' ta his mama as if she was there and pickin' up shells to see if they was vacant or not. We figured he couldn't go nowhere, so we kept on without him.

When we got to the bridge, we saw there was no way of crossin' it. Folks from town had come from the south bridge and said the same. Weren't no help comin' for nobody that day. We needed to help ourselves. Sorta went on callously, lookin' through the dead, hopin' ta find your daddy among the livin'. As we got inta town, I was surprised a few structures had held out against nature. There was a little girl sittin' in the sand, naked. The wind had taken the roof off of her house, and her family had watched her be sucked up and out of the house. Somehow, she had survived. Her skin was all pocked by the sand pelted against her body, and the same wind that had beaten her with sand had ripped the clothes off of her. Saw you in that little girl and had to help her. Took my wet shirt off and wrapped it 'round her, scooped her up and went to go find her some help, or at least to find her family. Took a while. That family had lost so many members during the storm, and they was distraught searchin' the island for who was left. Givin' their little girl back to them gave me hope, so I kept searchin' for your daddy.

Walked the island through the daylight hours. Searchin', cryin' out. Found lots of bodies. The bodies in the trees were left for that day. They was all sorts of folks. Men, women— the wind didn't care. Modest townswomen stuck in the trees with all of their goods displayed for anyone who walked by down below. Weren't nothin' we could do for them that day. That first day was for findin' the livin'. A guy was found on the ground. One of the trucks had blown over on him and got stuck upside down like. He'd managed to flinch just right and crawl inta a window. Don't know how the water missed takin' him, but it did. There were a few folks like that the first day. Miracles saved from the wrath of the storm. Weren't your daddy though. I wanted to believe he was still alive, stuck in some tree somewhere, but all I was findin' in trees was bodies, and I knew your daddy woulda found a way back. That night, as I sat down wet and tired from a day of searchin', I knew we wasn't findin' your daddy and there was nothin' I could do about it.

The next day, the sun rose like it didn't have a care in the world, just a shinin' on us as we started the job of clearin' the dead that was bakin' and swellin' in the sun. Some of the townsfolk was concerned about the amount of bodies. Musta been hundreds of 'em; the worry was they was gonna spread disease and infect the water table. The concerns seemed valid, so we started pilin' up the bodies in town to burn 'em, sort of like a funeral pyre, we decided. All those guys I'd buried along the Front, they at least got a marker. These guys were just gonna be burned and all that would be left would be a list of who'd been burned, which meant we had to try and identify their broken and twisted faces. Weren't no help comin'; with the bridge bein' down, help'd have to come on boats, and while the government weren't in no hurry to get down there in boats, the Conchs were. Florida folks know how to help each other after a hurricane and didn't figure they needed to wait for no government to tell them to do it.

Hemingway was one of the first to come. He pulled in with his boat. Weren't no docks left so he had to anchor and wade in. Didn't matter none that he was a famous author then. He was one of us. He knew some of the bodies he was helpin' ta pull bloated from the water. One of the guys he pulled out was one of the same men he'd bought drinks for in Key West just a few days before. Sorta broke him like it did the rest of us, seein' all the men who'd died cuz they had nowhere to hide from the storm, and no way of retreatin'. It was just like trench warfare. No real place to hide from the enemy, and no way to retreat—just left to fight or die.

These were things I thought of later. That day was for clearin' the dead. We worked together to get them down from trees. Had to start chasin' birds off of the bodies. It was bad enough they would only get a funeral pyre, and no proper burial, weren't no animals gonna get at them.

A few days passed like that before help came. We cleared bodies by day, and by night we sat on the shoreline and slept in the sand. Weren't much to eat or drink, we kinda moved on without thinkin', numb-like. The fires burned for days and brought back a smell from the front that I had hoped not to smell again. Gets in your clothes and your hair. Some of the guys would try to wash it out in the waves after, but they was still findin' bodies washin' in, so I chose to stink. You get used to it after a while.

When official help finally came, we started to learn more

about how bad the damage really was. The light house had all the windows broken by the wind. The wind alone—nothin' was blowin' inta those windows. Some boat sank off near the Rebecca Light with all the folks in it. No bodies found. Government figured they had life jackets on and floated out to sea. As the days passed, we also started gettin' more of an idea of how many men we'd lost across all of the islands. Thing was, they was only countin' the bodies that were found, not the men whose bodies couldn't be found. Didn't take no count of the bridges bein' washed out, 'long with the train tracks. No idea how they thought these men had just gone off on their own. They still said there was only about 250 of us vets gone. I argued with those pencil pushers that the number was much higher, that those guys that was gone had washed out, just like the ones on the boat, but the government guys said that the missin' vets was probably off drinkin' somewhere's. No account drifters they called 'em, or somethin' like that. Got me three days in the clinker that statement did. Couldn't listen to some fat ass sittin' in a chair tellin' me my brother was a no good, no account off drinkin' somewhere's and he'd show up later. I watched him wash away. Didn't matter none, and apparently punchin' the government man is frowned on. I thought at the time it was worth it, but truth was I just lost a few days of lookin' for the lost. Not that it woulda mattered none.

In the days after, I wandered all the islands. Spent weeks gettin' ta every corner I could get to. Talkin' ta anyone I could find who'd found a body. Givin' your daddy's facial deformities from the gas in France and his left hand bein' gone, I figured maybe someone would remember findin' him. No one matchin' his description'd been found.

After some time, I had to let him go. Truth is, I'd known from that first moment when his arm slipped from mine, he was gone. There was nothin' I could do 'bout it, but I've been feelin' the weight of his death. It shoulda been me there on the end, the one the water took. Mil shoulda been the one next to the man with the iron grip. That guy woulda kept Mil in the train. Mil didn't have no left hand to hold on to the bar with in that train—why did I leave him on the end by the bar? That's the question's been goin' round my mind ever since. Got used to him bein' able to do everything any other man could do with two hands, and to do it better with his one hand. Boy could he grip with that left nub. Guy could lift hay bales, make mash, and work the gilnets like no man's business; didn't cross my mind that he couldn't grip that bar in the storm. Didn't even think about it, truth be told. It was like the water knew, and after weeks of searchin', I had to give up on findin' what was left of your daddy.

Once I gave up, I knew I needed to head home. Figured they thought both of us was dead, bein' as how they hadn't heard from us since before the storm. Government weren't sendin' home no notifications for those whose bodies weren't found. Figured they was out drinkin' somewhere's and they'd show up when they was good and ready, so no need to notify the families. That job fell on me. Took my time headin' north. I'd spent enough time in a train for one lifetime, so I wasn't takin' no train. Walked most of the way. Took some time in the 'Glades. Fished and talked to other guys was moonshinin' during Prohibition. We fished and talked. One of 'em helped me get a bit further by water. Most folks just let me be. Weren't real interested in what I was doin', less I was walkin' by their piece of land, and then they was sure to watch me go by. I let 'em watch. Maybe they was jealous of your uncle Will's beard. I hadn't shaved since the storm, and it was October so it was gettin' ta be quite a sight, but guessin' by how dirty and ragged I was, they was probably thinkin' other thoughts. No matter. I kept on goin'. Took me 'bout three months to get back. Got arrested again, 'round 'bout Apopka. I was hungry. Hadn't right well eaten in days, and there was this there pie just a sittin' in a window just askin' ta be eaten, and eat it I did. It was one of them juicy fruit pies. Sure did taste good . . . not as good as your mama's though, or miss Rosie's. I'd'a givin' anything to be home eatin' their cookin', but given my reason for headin' home, I weren't in no particular hurry.

That night in prison, though, it was my first and only night in a actual jail, weren't too bad. In the Keys, they'd had a makeshift jail seein' as how the real one'd washed away. It was a different experience bein' in a real jail. Felt somethin' like a real criminal. But they fed me dinner, which is what I was after, and the next mornin' they drove me outta town and told me not to come back that a way. Well, seein' as I was headin' north and I was hungry, I remembered the town of Apopka with a certain fondness. None of the other towns fed me and drove me on my way. Saw them as sorta helpin' me out, and I kept on goin'.

After a while, my shoes gave out. Didn't take long, really, 'bout the time I hit Tampa. Thought of takin' a pair from a porch, but while I could see fit to take a pie here and there, couldn't take no man's shoes. I knew from my daddy how much a pair of shoes means to a man. Can't work most jobs without a pair of shoes. Every man needs one good pair and that's it. Add a pair of overalls and you's all set. Well, couldn't take a man's way of walkin' ta earn his livelihood, so I kept on walkin' bare foot. Now us kids had walked near about everywhere bare foot, but that was nothin' compared to walkin' up the state with no shoes on. By the time I reached Rosie's, my feet was torn to shreds, and I was bleedin'. Must of been quite a sight. Rosie didn't mind none, she never did. She came a runnin' out to see me in the road. Left her customers sittin' at their tables and just hugged me right in the street. They all thought me and your daddy was both gone for. Rosie took me inta the kitchen, set some coffee and chicken in front of me and knelt down to clean and bandage my feet. I just sat and listened to her talk. Couldn't bring myself to tell her what I had seen in the Keys, or what had happened to your daddy. She seemed to know, either by the look of me or cuz she knew us well enough to know I wouldn't'a left your daddy nowhere.

As it turns out, that there storm didn't stop at the Keys. That was all I'd heard, but then again, I wasn't really listenin', just lookin' for your daddy. Rosie knelt there cleanin' my cuts and tellin' me how that storm hit the Gulf of Mexico and turned. Looped itself right 'round and hit Cedar Key, if you can believe that. Well, guess you was old enough that you probably remember it goin' overhead. Did some damage in Cedar Key, but you and your mama was livin' in Chiefland still, your mama was helpin' Rosie again and makin' ends meet for the two of you. Two mamas helpin' ta raise their babies with no daddies. Chiefland didn't see too much from that storm in the higher areas, just in the areas that lined the river and other marshy areas. Your mama knew better than to have you near a marshy area. Too much sickness and skeeters.

Not everyone was safe. While we was in the Keys workin', Josh was up in Gainesville workin' at the segregated camp. Figured work was work, and he'd take it even if it was segregated work. Not many was hirin' then. Beggars can't be choosers, and that's where Josh felt he was at, even though the man had served his nation and earned the nickname "Harlem Hellfighter" from the enemy, the man weren't worth nothin' when he got back, but I guess none of us was.

Just like the camp in the Keys, the segregated camp was in a low place in Gainesville. Lots of marshlands in Gainesville at that point, and it didn't take much to wash away the shacks the government had built those men. Only one man died in the whole city that day, and Rosie cried when she told me it was Josh. Josh was the only guy I had left, and the storm took him, too. Washed away and weren't worth more than a blip in the Gainesville paper. Didn't even have much family left to mourn him. I wasn't there, so even though there was a body, only one or two of his extended family was there to see him placed in a common, unmarked grave. That's the way it worked. Man was a vet and a hero, left to drown like we was, and then thrown in a pit without so much as a marker for me to visit. Wasn't sure what to do after Rosie was done tellin' me. Weren't nothin' I could do for Josh or your daddy now. Knew I had to go tell your mama but didn't right know how. Seemed the whole world had crashed down 'round me and weren't much left to live for, and that is where more of my regret lies, Anne. I shoulda seen I had you to live for. Had myself convinced I wasn't no good for you, couldn't help you and your mama none.

As always, Rosie knew what to do when I didn't. She put me to bed in my usual spot on her porch, got me a blanket and pillow and everything. Knows how to spoil a man, that girl does. She went and got your mama and told her I was home and your daddy was gone. Your mama thought he was gone, but findin' out she was right didn't help none. Rosie told me later your mama just about melted inta a puddle and lay on the floor cryin'. You woke up from bed and came and lay on the floor with her, holdin' her and cryin'. You hadn't heard Rosie talkin', but you knew from your mama cryin' your daddy weren't comin' home.

Rosie took the brunt of it for me. She took the heavy tears and the cryin'. Just sat with your mama as long as she needed. Left her boy at home to keep an eye on me, in case I needed anything or maybe to keep me from runnin' off 'fore I could tell them more of the story. Knew everyone would want to know the details of how he died and where he was buried. Ricky's son was a young man 'bout that time, and he wouldn't'a had a problem keepin' me there, if it'd come to that, but I slept all night and didn't even know Rosie had left. First time I had a safe place to lay my head since before the storm.

In the mornin', I woke up with the three of you girls comin' on the porch. No one asked me nothin', but you two fell on me cryin' and huggin' me. The three of us sat there cryin' and talkin' 'bout your daddy while Rosie made us some corn cakes and coffee. After we ate, I knew ya'll were wantin' ta know how your daddy died. I left out some'a the details. Couldn't bring myself to tell you 'bout the worst parts, figured you needed to know what it was like, how it was with the storm, and that your daddy was gone. I seen him wash outta that train—that was what you needed to know, or so I thought then. Told you 'bout all the guys with no bodies left behind and how we was lookin' for guys for days. Your mama asked me why no one notified her of your daddy's death, and I told her 'bout how the government decided he weren't really gone, musta walked away drinkin' somewhere. Think that was my big mistake, one of the many, I suppose. Your mama, she knew your daddy was gone. For all his faults, she knew he would never walk away from her and from me. She knew your daddy, really knew him, since we was kids. Woman never wavered in her faith that your daddy was gone. But you was just a kid. You knew your daddy left months before, but since you didn't know why, you figured he left like other guys did. You knew he'd been drinkin', you knew he'd left. That was all you felt you needed to know. Your mama, bein' the lady she was, never told you the truth 'bout her finger, and I'm guessin', if she's readin' this, she ain't happy with me for tellin' you now. But it's time—time for you to know your daddy, so you know he didn't leave. He never woulda left 'cept ta provide for his family and to get back to bein' the daddy he felt you deserved. He left for you and your mama, and nothin' woulda ever stopped him from gettin' back to you. Nothin' but a hurricane.

CHAPTER TWENTY-SIX

Lost in Translation

Felt lost after that. Didn't right know where to turn. Went back to the shack Josh and I had shared years before. Felt good to be alone with myself and the fish. Sat out there for months, I suppose. Weren't really watchin' the time pass, just woke up when the sun did, fished, and went to bed when the sun did. Ricky's daddy showed up with a canoe one day. Didn't say nothin'. Just nodded, gave me the canoe and left. Gesture meant a lot to me. Gave me the chance to really disappear. Went off in that canoe and hopped from island to island. Went to our island, Anne. Visited the graves you and I visited all those years ago. Funny that the government thought your daddy was driftin' seein' as they didn't find him, but it was me that ended up driftin'.

When I was done fishin' for myself, I went down towards Tampa. Heard some of the guys was down that way and figured I could get a job with the Greeks spongin'. Those guys didn't care none how much we drank or how we looked. Me and the guys could dive and hold our breath longer than most. No fear of death—that was the secret. People panic under water and head to the top for air 'cuz they's afraid of runnin' outta air and dyin'. Me and the guys that came from the camp wasn't afraid to die, so we was good spongers. Went down and stayed down 'til we had what we went lookin' for.

Didn't speak Greek, so didn't make many friends, but I wasn't there for makin' friends. Spent my time with the guys, drinkin' and laughin'. Didn't talk none 'bout the Keys, and it didn't matter. Sometimes we bought friends in town with our paychecks, but you don't want to hear 'bout that.

Had my fortieth birthday out there along the coast in Tampa. Didn't tell no one it's was my day, but somehow those guys found out, some of the girls from town, too. Set me up a table in the bar along the water. Reminded me of Sloppy Joe's in Key West. One of the girls brought me some homemade pie. Knew I had a soft spot for fruit pie ever since my trip up the coast. We sat there and saw the sun set, the dolphins herdin' fish inta the sea wall and feastin'. Ain't never seen nothin' like it in all my time in Cedar Key. Sure, we saw dolphins in Cedar Key workin' together to catch fish, but never seen 'em usin' a wall to trap those fish. Sure did show how smart those oversized fish were. Anyway, 'bout that time one'a the guys said we should fish. The water weren't too deep over the sea wall, and we was in the water all day anyways. The guy behind the bar had some poles he said he'd lend us if we shared some fish with him. He knew us well enough to know we would catch some fish, and let me tell you, we was just a throwin' 'em outta the water. Girls were puttin' 'em in a bucket from the bar. We was all laughin', and not thinkin'. See, the sun was settin' and normally we didn't get in no sea water when the sun set, seein' as that was when the sharks came out to play. We didn't play with their kind, unless a big knife was involved. Well, in all the fun, we didn't think 'bout the time, the sun, or the dolphins leavin'. See, dolphins will attack sharks, so generally sharks don't mess with 'em. When you are surrounded by dolphins, you can pretty much take it as a sign there ain't no sharks 'round. But the dolphins had left, and we didn't notice 'til I was 'bout waste deep in the water, reelin' in a big one, and when it finally broke the surface, there was only half of him left. A big 'ol shark'd eaten half of him right off my line. Figured it was time to get back over the sea wall and inta our bar stools. Boy did we laugh though, and we ate good too, between the pie and the fish. The bar keep sent the fish back to the kitchen and fried our share up right quick. Fried fish, beer, and pie. Didn't get much better than that at the time.

What I shoulda done at this point was head back up to you and your mama, but didn't figure there was a place for me, and there were too many ghosts in town. Figured I'd keep headin' south when I didn't want to sponge no more. Went 'round Apopka outta respect for the free meal they'd given me those years ago. Found the camp that'd helped me in the Glades. They was more than willin' ta take me on again, seein' as I could catch and skin a gator like no man. All those times runnin' from the law as a kid, I knew how to dodge the man and bring in as many gators as was needed. Fished for myself, and sometimes I caught more to sell. Set myself up real nice down there in the Glades. No one asked me questions, and I didn't go 'round talkin'. They caught on real quick I had skills they needed, whether it was hidin' from the man or brewin' some home brew, I was their man.

Fell in with a woman 'bout that time. Her man was gone. Not sure what from. So many died, got to where I didn't ask. I brought home the food for her and her littles, and she cooked and cleaned for me. Weren't much more to the relationship than that. We both needed each other, and we got what we needed. Lived that way for a year or two, fishin', poaching' and brewin'. Guess that's why I found out 'bout my sickness. It's just like a woman to push a man to go to the doctor. Wouldn't'a gone otherwise. Things had been off for a while. My skin was even lookin' unnatural and yella. She noticed before me, even though we weren't particularly close. Ours was a relationship of convenience, so to speak. We was helpin' each other through, not much more.

Well, she was right to send me. Doc took one look at me and asked me how much I've been drinkin' and for how long.

I told him enough and for as long as I wanted to. I've never really been one for conversation. He ran some test and had me come back for the results. That's more times than I'd been to the doctor in my life, aside from havin' the flu in boot camp. Well, found out right quick that I wasn't makin' it outta this one. My liver was ruined, and it was my fault. Told me I might get a year or two if'n I'd stop drinkin, but even that woman knew that wasn't gonna happen. Told her I'd move along, didn't want her kids to watch me drinkin' myself to death, seein' as we both now knew that was what I was doin'. Set 'em up with some chopped wood before I left. Weren't an easy task in a swamp, oddly enough. Got their ice box filled with fish, too, and then I took off. Wouldn't be long 'fore she would replace me with some younger, healthier guy. Weren't much I had to offer that most those Glades guys couldn't offer, and man could she cook. Knew I didn't need to feel no remorse for her and her kids. I decided I wanted to die where your daddy did. Seemed right, seein' as we was twins and all. Probably shoulda headed back to you, but there's somethin' funny 'bout findin' out your dyin'. Seems to switch somethin' in your head. All the sudden, I realized how tired I was. Didn't think I could make it up to ya'll walkin' and didn't have no other way of gettin' there. Still not takin' trains. Don't own no car. So, I walked on down to the Keys. Didn't take too long, not like walkin' up the state to ya'll. Fell back in with the guy in town that'd leant your daddy books back in the day. He wasn't happy to see me like this but was glad I'd come to him. Gave me a job keepin' his lawn up and let me sleep out back in his shed. His wife has been feedin' me. Think they know what's goin' on, even though I haven't told 'em.

It's felt right bein' here. I can feel your daddy here, lookin' out at the water from the same ground we used to sit on, lookin' at the fire and laughin' with the guys. Most nights I sit here and watch the sun set. The best nights I spend here are sittin' and smokin' while watchin' that fiery ball sink into the sea. The last few years I spent runnin' from my memories, but now it's time to sit and think through them. I knew I needed to share them all with you. Most of them your mama knew, some of them you knew, but from a little girl's perspective. Childhood warps memories. I need you to see how things were, even back before your mama.

CHAPTER TWENTY-SEVEN

The End

Well, Anne, I'm runnin' out of paper. I've written it all down for you. You see, the doctor is sayin' now I've not got much time. Says it's my own fault. It's still my fault and I won't stop it. I've been walkin' 'round with grief and alcohol for too long to let go of either, but I made my peace with heaven, and I accept my fate. Most everyone I've loved has already passed that way, some of 'em violently and in front of my eyes. There's nothin' left for me to fear.

Your daddy helped me make my peace, 'though it took me a few years to accept. Like I said, when your daddy and I were in that camp in the Keys, he started comin' 'round, was readin' poetry again and writin' like he was before. Well, one poem he really liked was by Francis somebody. Real, real long poem. I couldn't sit through the whole thing like your daddy could. The beginning went like this:

> I fled him, down the nights and down the days
> I fled him, down the arches of the years;
> I fled him down the labyrinth ways of my own mind

I liked that part. There's been so much hangin' on my mind, all of which you now know, but anyways, it was later lines that got me:

> From those strong feet that followed, followed after . . .
> Heaven and I wept together . . .
> All of which thy child's mistake
> Fancies as lost, I have stored for thee at home
> Rise, clasp my hand and come! . . .
> I am He who thou fearest

I can still hear your daddy readin' those lines to the guys 'round the campfire. All the guys in the camp liked to hear him read. T'weren't much around to read, but he always found somethin'. Well those lines stuck with me and now I can say that Jesus forgave the shit outta me. He followed me and waited. He cried with me—everything I lost is with him.

Now, I'm not sayin' all this to ask for your forgiveness. I

don't deserve that. I'm askin' you to see your daddy. See him for the boy, the soldier, the husband, and the father he was. See him and forgive him. With that bein' said, goodbye, Anne. Bury me where you see fit.

EPILOGUE

My grandfather, Pvt Leon Henry Hughes, whose life helped to fill in gaps for Will and Mil's characters, returned home and eventually married my grandmother, a woman so wonderful he could never have been worthy. He raised both of his sons to grow up and serve the country in the military. Given his birth in 1895, he died before I was able to know him. According to comments that appear to be about him in his local CCC camp newsletter, he was a good dancer. That cannot be confirmed.

Rosie. Rosie is a powerhouse. She worked her way through her undergraduate degree as a single mother at the University of Florida, where she met Tim Tebow at the beginning of his career and told him "good luck with that football thing." She has since earned a Masters and one day I believe she will run a VA. She is unstoppable. Her heart is for the veterans in her VA and she works tirelessly to help them. She spends much of her free time with other Gold Star moms and is her son's biggest champion.

The conclusion I draw from the lives, both fictional and non-fictional, of Rosie, Caleb, Ricky, and my grandfather, is that we will never deserve our veterans. They are truly the best our nation has to offer. While we do not deserve them, we must try to serve them better by accepting them as they are, by trying to help where we can and by voting for politicians who will enact laws for better support of the men and women who come home changed or broken from war. Reconsideration should also be given for the politicians and military heroes who are responsible for the deaths of WWI veterans on US soil. Patton, FDR, and MacArthur need to be remembered not just for the good they have done, but also for the brutal treatment given to the Bonus Army and the neglect of the WPA camp in the Keys.

NOTES

For more information on Patton, MacArthur and Eisenhower's roles in the Bonus Army, see the following:

- Dickson, Paul and Thomas B. Allen. *The Bonus Army: An American Epic*. Walker and Company, New York. 2004.

For more information on the Labor Day Hurricane of 1935 or the Rosewood massacre, see the following:

- Drye, Willie. *Storm of the Century: the Labor Day Hurricane of 1935*. National Geographic, Washington, DC. 2002.

- Gonzalez-Tennant, Edward. *The Rosewood Massacre: An Archeology and History of Intersectional Violence*. University Press of Florida. 2018.

- Scott, Phil. *The Great Florida Keys Storm of 1935: Hemingway's Hurricane*. McGraw Hill. 2006.

The following poems are quoted in the designated chapters. All are in the public domain and can be found readily online or in the following collections:

Chapter five:
- Donne, John. "The Flea." *The Top 500 Poems*. William Harmon, ed. Columbia University Press, 1992. 141.

Chapter nine:

- Cressy, Will M. "God Help America to Help God Save the King." *War Poems*. Gabriel-Meyerfield, Co. 13

- Whitman, Walt. "O Captain! My Captain!" *The Top 500 Poems*. William Harmon, ed. Columbia University Press, 1992. 692-693.

Chapter seventeen:

- The poem in chapter seventeen can be found on a grave in an abandoned grave yard in an island off of Cedar Key by those who know where to look and are willing to fight hordes of mosquitos to see it.

Chapter eighteen:

- McKay, Claude. "If We Must Die." *The Top 500 Poems*. William Harmon, ed. Columbia University Press, 1992. 998.

Chapter twenty-two:

- Kipling, Rudyard. "Danny Deever" *The Top 500 Poems*. William Harmon, ed. Columbia University Press, 1992. 851.

- The French song is called La Chanson de Craonne or The Song of Craonne. It is also known as Adieu la Vie or Goodbye to Life. It was written as an anti war song by French soldiers of WWI.

Chapter twenty-four:

- Owen, Wilfred. "The End." *Above the Dreamless Dead: World War I in Poetry and Comics*. Chris Duffy, ed. First Second, New York. 2014. 116-119.

Chapter twenty-seven:

- Thompson, Francis. "The Hound of Heaven." *The Top 500 Poems*. William Harmon, ed. Columbia University Press, 1992. 843-848.

For more information on veterans transitioning back into a civilian world, see the documentary produced by Marine Corps veteran Jonathan Hancock *Bastards' Road*, which is available to stream on Amazon.

A Brother's Story

CPSIA information can be obtained
at www.ICGtesting.com
Printed in the USA
BVHW030515080322
630868BV00001B/29